Carts and Other Stories

Zdravka Evtimova

Fomite
Burlington, Vermont

ISBN-13: 978-1-937677-02-2

Library of Congress Control Number: 2011944245
Fomite
58 Peru Street
Burlington, VT 05401
www.fomitepress.com

Cover Art - Ethan Azarian (www.ethanazarian.net)
Author Photo - Diana Ivanova

Carts and Other Stories

Contents

Gosho

"Don't waste time. Come to my place quickly! I'll treat you to a piece of Gosho as soon as you arrive," my friend Dara called me on my mobile. I listened, hesitating. Yesterday, my husband bought a big knife and said he'd use it to slash my throat. I wasn't too impressed to be honest with you. Let me first explain the way the whole picture looked.

Gosho was a 21-year-old donkey whose proud proprietor was Dara's father, Uncle Pesho. The man prepared his cart, then took Gosho and went to steal tiles, scrap iron, sawdust, plus everything else one could lay his hands on in these parts. I was one of the few who knew the truth about the old donkey and I didn't take pride in that knowledge. To cut a long story short, it was Uncle Pesho himself who turned Gosho into minced meat and subsequently into sausages. I was well informed about the substantial role these sausages played in our small town.

Uncle Pesho was stealing scrap iron when Gosho fell on his belly and started hiccuping and sighing. Then suddenly the animal's back stopped twitching.

"Why are you doing that to me, man?" Uncle Pesho said to his beast. "Who shall I steal with now? My wife is an old rail like the rusty ones at the railway station. My daughter (he meant Dara, of course), will never get married because no one wants her. The two geese are both so lazy they'd rather kick the bucket than do a stroke of work. I am old and worn out like your horseshoes, Gosho, but I go filching. Can't I get a drink like an honest man instead? And what can I steal, my friend? Everything worth stealing has already been stolen. I go out thieving and who do you think I meet? I meet my competitors. They've gone out to pilfer something or other, too. So what happens when I see them eye to eye, I ask you? Do we steal the way we should? Not at all! We all sit down and get drunk together. Tell me, Gosho, didn't I give you a chunk of my bread all the time? I did! So don't die, man. Are you leaving me with the slothful female pair, with the old one and the young one? Are you? You can't die now!"

But Gosho kicked weakly and stuck out his tongue at his master. Uncle Pesho was in a quandary. A donkey that weighed more than two hundred pounds should not meet his maker like that! Imagine more than two hundred pounds of edible meat dying under your nose while the refrigerator in your house was as empty as your pocket. No way.

I didn't know if Gosho died first and then Uncle Pesho slit his throat with his penknife, or Gosho was slaughtered first and then passed away. As far as I knew, he'd rather cut Dara's throat. (*That hen doesn't get married anyway. She just gapes at the TV all day long. And why you think she does that: to learn something useful like making money? No, sir, not at all. She watches the stupid series and cries her eyes out. When her classmates come back from Italy or from Spain, all of them visit her and don't go out of her room for a week. At the end of the day none of them marries her. And her classmates are damned right if you ask me.)* In my opinion, Gosho must have died most respectably before he and his master stole the scrap iron, then Uncle Pesho cut his dead throat with his penknife. What I saw with my own eyes at long last were forty-two sausages, hanging under the eaves of Uncle Pesho's house. The man himself sat in a shabby armchair, a bottle of beer in his hand, unable to steal any more, tears in his eyes. He chewed at a piece of sausage, swilled down beer and wept for Gosho.

"Come quickly, you sleeping saucepan!" Dara, my best friend, called me on my mobile once again. "Hurry up. There's almost nothing left of Gosho."

I believed her. There was hardly anything left of Gosho and I knew the reason why: Dara had tried one of the sausages.

"It felt as if I gnawed on a paving stone," she told me later and I was sure that was true. Gosho was a very old donkey, may he rest in peace. Dara told me Uncle Pesho buried his ears not far from the Struma River. Whenever Aunt Dena, his wife, picked a quarrel with him, he went to Gosho's buried ears, drank beer and mourned. Even his competitors, the other thieves with carts, went and cried for the buried ears. They all remembered the way they had gotten drunk with Uncle Pesho.

When Dara tried Gosho's sausage for the first time, something quite unbelievable occurred. She met a guy by the name of Dancho. He was not one of her classmates, those who went to Italy and Spain and stayed in Bulgaria for no more than a week. He was a Bulgarian, every inch of him, and had never traveled far from his native village of Kralev. On account of that he didn't know anything about Dara's classmates and her inordinate love for the TV series.

"You are magnificent. I am happy," he told her after they met in one of the numerous cafés in our town. An hour later he said he wanted to introduce Dara to his mother. Dancho was 31 and Dara was 31 too, so they'd make a good couple, he said. Dara got scared and winked her eyes uncontrollably, unbelieving. She had got accustomed to being assured she was magnificent for no more than a week. Then the guys vanished. She dubbed them "classmates" for the sake of convenience although most of them were either ten years older or ten years younger than her. Generally speaking, plus or minus ten years didn't make a difference to Dara. The guy remained her *classmate*, and that meant that at the end of the week he collected all his shirts and socks and beat it for Italy or Spain.

Dancho, however, did something different. He paid a visit to Uncle Pesho and told him, "Dara is absolutely magnificent, you know. I can't find a more magnificent woman than her not only in my native village, but also in the capital of Bulgaria. So, if you don't mind, I'll marry her."

That statement rendered Dara speechless. Her classmates had said before, "We'll get married some day," but how could that festive event become reality when the bride was in Pernik, Bulgaria, while the bridegroom dillydallied in Madrid, Spain? Hardly possible at all.

Another friend of mine, Maria, tried Gosho's sausages too, although she felt a loathing for donkeys. You wouldn't believe what happened. On the following day she met a guy, Genady by name, on the train to Sofia. She was 34 and he was 32. Maria worked for the National Steel Industry Trust in an old workshop, so she could never trim her nails the way she'd liked. She, too, had a few classmates, but they were considerably less in number than Dara's; maybe because Dara was slim and tall while Maria rolled in her own lard. No matter what, that Genady guy from the train told her, "You are absolutely magnificent! I am thinner than my own shirt, but you are just what I've imagined a woman should be! I'd like to introduce you to my mother. I want to marry you."

And that was not all to the story about Gosho.

Unfortunately Aunt Dena, Uncle Pesho's wife, a quiet and perfectly normal fat woman, tried Gosho's sausages as well. Not that her teeth were that good, but as ill luck would have it, she got herself into trouble. She had a nibble at Gosho's sausages, and, of course, on the following day she was accosted by a funny sort of bloke as she sold stockings and T-shirts from her stall in the marketplace in Pernik. The guy had a shaggy disheveled beard and looked as strong as Uncle Pesho's bull. He told Aunt Dena, "You look magnificent to me," bought her a vanilla ice-cream, and in the afternoon he went to visit her in her house.

It was at that time when Uncle Pesho grabbed the same penknife with which he allegedly slaughtered Gosho and rushed to slit the bearded guy's throat. Unfortunately, the intruder was stronger than that bull in Pesho's pen. The newcomer bandied words with Uncle Pesho and the two men got into a fight. Aunt Dena watched them, grinning radiantly over the pot of vegetable soup that simmered on her kitchen stove.

Then still another friend of mine, Mira by name, tried Gosho's sausages, and on the following day, again on the morning train to Sofia, a fellow told her, "You are…"

You should guess what Dara did. She started selling Gosho's sausages at the price of 50 Euro a slice. If somebody expected that the price would frighten the ladies from Pernik, I'd tell him he'd never met a lady from Pernik in his life. Dara's house thronged with women. And they were not only 30-year-old beauties. There were 17-year-old girls. I saw 50-year-old ladies, 60-year-old matrons, and grandmothers with walking sticks. I noticed a girl from the elementary school with a 50 Euro bill in her hand.

That was the reason why Dara called me on my mobile for a third time. "Hey, sleeping saucer!" she said. "You've got to get moving. Soon there will be nothing left of Gosho and you'll rot like an apple in a pantry."

Dara was my next-door neighbor and she could very well listen every time my husband Tosho and I had quarrels over money. Apart from being in total disagreement about the way I should spend our income, I got into arguments with Tosho on a number of other issues. He had warned me he liked the waitress in the local eatery, so I'd better watch out for him. He said also he was sick and tired of me. He implied he could at any minute beat it for Spain, but at the same time he underlined that he'd bought a knife to do me in if I tried a piece of Gosho's sausages.

The men who owned old donkeys, all of them from the group of Uncle Pesho's competitors, took their beasts to the same locale near the Struma River and cut the animal's throats. They even borrowed Uncle Pesho's penknife, paying him 8 Euro an hour. None of these guys had a beast of burden any more, so the scrap iron and the tiles remained unattended. The sausages from their donkeys failed to bring anyone saying to a girl, "You are magnificent."

"You silly saucepan," Dara scolded me on my mobile. "I keep one piece of Gosho especially for you. Your husband is as lazy as Gosho's buried ears, and he's got a roving eye. He doesn't have two pennies to rub together, does he? Don't waste time. Come quick and eat that piece of Gosho's sausage. You have one child, and you'll bring her up this way or other. Take my word, Tosho doesn't care for you. Why should you put up with him, you fool? You get fatter and he knows it."

"Okay," I said. "I'm coming."

Before I set out for Dara's place, I threw the biggest knife in our house in the Struma River. It was the same weapon my husband had bought from the marketplace, the one with which he intended to do me in. I had hardly taken a couple of steps when I saw my husband Tosho. It was obvious he hadn't found the big knife that rusted in the mud of the Struma River. He'd grabbed an ax instead.

"If you go and eat that sausage, I'll cut your head off here and now!"

"Oh, will you?" I said. "I'm curious how you'll do that. Even if I remained headless, I'd go and eat that sausage. You'd better remember that very well."

Then Tosho hurled the ax on the ground and shouted, "You are magnificent. You are the only magnificent woman among all women I know. I tell you the honest truth and you don't have to go and eat that damned sausage. Let me be cold and dead like Gosho if I'm lying to you!"

Dara's father and the rest of his competitors, who didn't have donkeys any more, drank brandy together in the café across from our house.

"Hey, Tosho," they yelled. "Why are you telling her she's magnificent? Don't you have eyes in your head, man?"

Endless July

Perhaps I behave so foolishly on account of my confused childhood and the endless July evenings when I was alone with my enormous mass.

The trucks loaded with scrap iron would roar at night, reeking of diesel, shaking the windows with the reverberating sound of their engines, and I could not sleep. I had the feeling that a line of two hundred trucks crept along my aorta and would burst into my heart—I had always imagined it was a defective organ that would put its owner in jeopardy. The trucks were my father's; he was ruining himself to make a bright future for me, exporting pig iron from the metallurgy plant in the town, importing scrap iron—meaning heaps of rusty iron wires stolen every now and then from different places. In general, he was killing himself quite successfully. A few thugs had shot at him a couple of times. He was no lesser a thug than they were, but he had a convincing excuse: he loved his fat daughter very much. But why should he love me? I was a greasy bulldozer for whom the seamstresses had to sew special jeans into which a hippopotamus could comfortably crawl.

Bombs exploded twice in front of our house. On one of the occasions my mother's upper arm was wounded: a scratch. She then spent twenty-five days in the hospital.

After that incident she left us and went to live with the doctor who had healed her wound. My mother was a very beautiful woman with green eyes that contained falling oak leaves in autumn and sprouting oak trees in spring. Actually, there was a whole calendar in her eyes, but it wasn't so much her eyes as her endless legs that compelled the doctor to fall head over heels for her. I have inherited her green eyes, but in my case they are almost always invisible under the hills of fat that surround them. I have inherited something from my father as well—he was enormous, with a broad back and a popping belly.

My mother left us before the trucks started rumbling at night. After she ran off with all her belongings and boxes and bottles of make up, Daddy made up his mind to become the biggest, richest player in town so mother would drown in a lake of misery asking herself why she had cut the throat of the hen that would have laid golden eggs for her.

My father could read a little and was quite familiar with the multiplication table, which was just enough for his business. Perhaps it was the hardness of his skull that made him the proud proprietor of two hundred completely different trucks with which he sold iron, cucumbers, potatoes, condoms, medicines, and the rest. Mother used to tell the story of how, before she married my father, other guys used to beat him up at least twice a week. Later, she seemed to take a certain twisted pleasure in this memory, seeing nothing in the man she married, that enormous semi-literate oaf, but a swamp of love and sympathy for me, with nothing left over for her. That must have made

her furious. I was his only child and had heavy breasts under which the greasy pillow of my belly began; bellow it
my gigantic thighs jutted out, jiggling like bowls of soup.
Let me not speak of my behind whose volume probably
put to shame that of the sand in the Sahara.

For quite a while my swollen body didn't get me into
trouble; even when we were poor my father left rolls of
one hundred dollar bills in the drawer of the kitchen table.
He never counted them, saying the money was mine.
Mother, whose name was Kalina - (I guess her name hasn't
changed yet), used to nod her head enviously remarking
that the wad of bills in her drawer was smaller than the
one in mine.

She had everything. The best massage expert in town,
Maria by name, came to take care of her beautiful figure.
The most distinguished beautician was responsible for her
face—the most famous artist in Pernik, a bearded phony
with a bald head and the manners of a well trained pug,
had already drawn seven pictures of my mother in different poses. Her flesh twinkled on the canvas, and my father
would rush towards her, with his eyes first, then with his
body, flowing hurriedly to her. She was a shrewd woman,
my mother was.

She got a degree in law from the local university even
before she left us and started integrating herself into the
cultural elite of the town. Perhaps she is integrating herself perfectly in the house of her new husband; Doctor
Xanov was one of the richest surgeons in the region,
younger than she was and very tall. He worked in Pirogov

hospital,[1] had a staggeringly large number of private patients on his list, and, unlike my father, he never swore.

Doctor Xanov made great efforts to diminish the fat under my skin; he was unaware of the fact that my lard thawed whenever I looked at him. My father often fought with other guys when brandy turned his brains into soup. Even when his chauffeurs, time and again, brought him home bashed, thrashed, and very bloody, he looked at me as if I weren't a fat, female colossus but the most beautiful girl in the world. Sometimes, in the evenings, he used to put his enormous hand on my head. His palm was the size of a small pillow and had an indefinite number of notches, scars, and wounds from his fights, but on my head it felt smoother than honey. My father didn't say anything, just looked at me, peacefully. I suppose he might have felt sorry for me, for he knew women well, and felt that a fat one like me had no chance whatsoever. He simply loved me as a dog loves his puppy even when it is ugly.

In happier days, when the guys brought Dad home drunk and squashed after his regular sprees, Doc Xanov would come to our house to patch him up. Of course, he got juicy fees for his services. My mother helped and did her best handing him bandages, little squares of gauze, or disinfectant. It was perhaps at that time that they fell in love; however that was not the subject of my curiosity. It is curious for me that, after my father was shot, Doctor Xanov and my mother stood by my side at his funeral,

---

[1] Pirogov Hospital - the National emergency hospital in Bulgaria

looking so sad, as if they both suffered from a splitting toothache.

It was at that time that Doctor Xanov let his hand drop on my shoulder; compared to my father's paw it felt like a slimy hen's beak pecking at my hair. Doctor Xanov's eyes were brown, the color of frozen leaves fallen long ago from their autumn branches that had just begun to decompose in the first warm days of spring.

As doctor Xanov examined me, he stuck his forefinger into the lard of my belly, showing my mother that the finger sunk in to the knuckle. His forefinger certainly did not sink into my mother's belly because her belly is flat and hard as brass. Her green eyes were of the same quality and that was why I avoided looking into them.

The police didn't find out who shot my father, and that was only natural. They almost never did unless you were some big shot whose widow would be willing to speak to the press about it. Mother was not at all willing to do that. Perhaps Father had thrashed and flogged many of his enemies, for before he died somebody set fire to the cafe he had built, and twice bombs exploded under his Mercedes. She might have been upset, but she didn't show it. Finally they killed him without dramatics; two bullets in the forehead and that was that.

Doctor Xanov thought I went off my hinges, but he didn't use those exact words when he diagnosed me. "A permanent shock" was how he put it. The truth was I was not scared of blood. At least once a week Father was brought home dripping and stained with blood. I suddenly was aware I would never again see his brown eyes that looked at me as if I were a perfectly normal seventeen- year-old girl. I would have done anything to make him come back to life.

He loved me as the sparrow loves its little sparrows, not with his brains (for is it possible for a human brain to love the equivalent of twenty-five frying pans of bacon?); he loved me with his blood, which had spilled and splashed onto the pavement.

My mother and father used to sleep in a spacious bedroom situated very far from my own but on the same floor of the house. In the middle of the night, I often heard screeching sounds and moans, so it was evident they made love. I would feel my blood howling in my ears. I would take a shower to cool the flaming lard of my body, but instead of getting cooler I had the impression that the water evaporated at the touch of my skin. The bathroom had mirrors on all its walls—mother had wanted it to be that way so that every square inch could reflect the perfection of her pearl-like body.

Sometimes I stayed with her while the masseuse labored diligently over her thighs, feeling transfixed, enchanted by her beauty. She looked at me with green jungle eyes with liana vines that strangled my throat. I could not imagine how she looked in the spacious bedroom with the marble floor and pictures drawn by dubious painters who pawned their splotchy works of art off on my father at incredible prices. How would he know what a good painting looked like?

My grandfather owns seven nanny goats and one cow; my father's mother, big and strong like the motor of a BMW car, herded the cow non-stop, silent, severe and grim. One day she remarked to my father gloomily, "She will be the death of you," meaning, of course, my mother.

I could not imagine mother under the silver canopy of their matrimonial bed; but she might have been very good for she conquered the most prestigious catch, Xanov the surgeon, seven years her junior.

Doctors, artists, and teachers in the provincial high school I attended fawned before my father. The brilliant female teachers in the private college I chose to study at did exactly the same because he paid them well to teach me the latest dances—rock-and-roll and tangos—me, under whose steps the parquet floor in the dance hall became unglued. My father couldn't spell the word "address" correctly, but he had all those rolls of one hundred dollar bills which were stronger than any doctor, policemen, or teacher; more powerful than the whole group labeled 'the elite'. He had money to burn. So did I.

I had never bought porno DVDs or porno magazines. I once found some Italian ones, which my mother kept at the bottom of her chest of drawers; I looked at them for no more than ten minutes. The next night I ran a temperature, felt giddy, and threw up. And that was not an insignificant event considering my imposing mass. It was that night that I made my decision: what I could not achieve by myself, my father's money would secure for me. How could I invite a man to my room considering the fact that in all the four suburbs of the town everybody worked for my father? The drivers of the 200 trucks, the petty scrap iron traders, the owners of car services, my father watched everything closely, businesses throve under his shadow, the city cops and the best lawyers worked for him. How would I find someone who didn't know my father—and how much would I have to pay him to keep it quiet?

My father had appointed a brawny man named Dancho for my personal chauffeur and he drove me in my jeep wherever I wanted to go. He was always with me, my shadow. Once my jeep was shot at because the attackers thought my father was inside. Bullets splintered Dancho's left shoulder destroying some nerves making his hand droop like a rag. He couldn't raise it to the steering wheel. He couldn't even make a fist. But he drove on, blood pouring from the wound, more concerned about what my father would do if he did not get me to safety than his own skin. Dancho was my body guard; he guarded it better than his own. It would not be easy escaping his shadow.

I would have to get out of our neighborhood of tall houses with courtyards and swimming pools. I could only find the man I needed where the eight-story flat buildings were; there lived the sacked workers from the steel combine that went bankrupt three years before. Most of the men were unemployed now. My father hired a few of the lucky ones and the rest stayed in the rooms of their small apartments in the daytime and got drunk in the evenings at "The Last Penny," a cheap pub run by my father where lousy alcohol was sold.

In those old blocks of flats I hoped to find my man. Although rumors about my father, and about me and my fat haunches, sprang up almost every day, and songs about Mother circulated—with the occasional pornographic lyric and inaccurate descriptions of her body parts—and flooded the town, the people from that area had never seen me in person.

I told Dancho that I was going to the town library, but I snuck my way to one of the dozens of little shops selling second-hand clothes. Most of the town's population bought their shirts and trousers from there, but who would ever think that the only daughter of Bloody Rayo would go shopping in the sleazy districts that smelled of sweat and urine? I dropped in at exactly eight neighborhoods like this and intentionally hung around in the sleaziest one; the cellar of one building was flooded. The water in it had turned into slime and pond scum, half of the first floor was abandoned, and in one of the remaining empty rooms there was a second-hand clothes shop. I guess it would be more accurate to say *fifteenth*-hand or *twentieth*-hand shop. It was evident that the shop assistant didn't recognize me.

She was very dark and there was dirt under her nails, her face was wrinkled and hidden below a layer of makeup some miles thick.

"What do you want?" she asked me, adding acidly, "You are very fat and I don't know if there are any clothes that will fit you."

"I'd like a skirt," I explained to her.

"Um, uh, you'd be lucky if I found any dress for you at

all. I haven't got a skirt that big. Try this dress on, but it is expensive, mind you. It's the only one I have that large." She wanted one lev[2] for the dress. For the first time in my life I was told that something that cost one lev was expensive. I paid her without any hesitation; the woman gave me a dragon's grin, causing the makeup to melt, and it flowed, mixed with sweat, down her cheeks towards her wrinkled neck. In a flash, she offered me two more dresses, as enormous as the previous one, but this time she said they cost ten levs apiece. She showed me a pair of shoes as well, so warped and torn that you could only use their heels to hit a stray dog on the head with or simply throw them in the trash.

"Wonderful merchandise," she boasted. "You can walk with these shoes for six years. They're already patched up so you won't need to bring them to a cobbler."

I did not buy the shoes. I chose a pair of slippers instead, which hardly clung to my heels, and gave her five levs for them. The woman grabbed at the money, stuck it right away in her bra and scratched her hand as if the bill had burned her skin. Then she jumped up, squeezed my arm, and dragged me to the upper floor; where she had "posh merchandise for big babes like you, love." She showed me a bathrobe mended in seven or eight places, worn and frayed as if a combat tank had driven over it several times. Then she unlocked a chest of drawers that was full of blouses— yellow, green, pink, and faded as if all that *posh* merchandise

---

[2] Bulgarian currency - 1 lev is equal to 65 American cents

18

had been soaked in sulfuric acid. "Five levs apiece," the woman announced generously without letting go my hand.

Her palm was very warm; then she took hold of my shoulder with both her hands and offered me a pair of underpants the size of a tent. I bought them for ten levs which made the woman gape at me. For maybe a whole minute she stood dumbfounded, then she hugged me and kissed my cheek.

"God bless you," she whispered, her mouth dripping with saliva. "God be with you every minute of your life!" At that very moment it dawned on me that I could ask if she knew of a guy for me.

"What's your name?" I asked. Suspicion shone immediately in her eyes, black and slippery like a skating rink.

"Why do you ask?"

"Because I want to come back to shop from you."

"My name's Natasha," she answered. "But my true Gypsy name is Fatma." I thought about the fact that I could buy all of her posh merchandise, the whole block of flats, the cellars of slime and mold with the smallest of the rolls of money my father had given me. The woman had sunk her black eyes into mine and refused to let go of my arm. "You want something else. I can tell that by looking at you."

"Listen, Fatma. Can you find a man for me?"

She went on plunging her eyes deeper into my head.

"You want a man?" she repeated slowly.

"Yes" I answered. Her eyes left mine and crept along the hills of my breasts, balanced on the greasy pillow of my belly, and then descended to my thighs. After that her hands let go of my shoulder, patted my stomach and back and, without any decorum whatsoever, groped my ass as if it were a vast unexplored part of the globe.

"You are fat," she clicked her tongue several times. "Very fat, I tell you. Tell me when you want to marry him and I'll tell you how much it will cost."

It was clear she had not understood. Her words made me shake as a result of which my belly and the cushions of lard above my waist wobbled like sacks stuffed with cabbage.

"You're really fat," she went on. "Are you sick? Is it some illness that makes you so fat?"

"I'm healthy."

"Then you eat too much. That's good. It means you have a lot of food at home. Don't you, eh? You bought so many things. I wish I were fat myself," she sighed and groped me once again, this time on my belly. "Can you breed?" she asked. I didn't answer. The whips of suspicion lashed me.

"Does your monthly blood flow regularly?" she added.

"Yes, it does."

"What sort of a guy do you want, scrawny or a fat one like you?"

"I'd like a skinny one. But..."

"What?"

"I don't want to marry him."

"What!" she hiccuped heavily then surveyed me carefully, her face underneath the makeup so deep in thought that the wrinkles stretched and shone like parallels and meridians on the globe of her cheeks. "Oh, yeah," she patted my arm once again and winked at me. "Oh, yeah. I'll bring a married man to you, and you'll give him something for his kids. He'll be pleased and you'll be pleased. Kiro has five children. You'll have to fetch two doughnuts for each kid. I know a bakery where they sell them cheap."

"No. I don't want a married man," I thought about my father, about me, my mother, and suddenly I was out of sorts imagining the children and the doughnuts from the cheap bakery. "I want to get to know a guy well," I lied to her.

"Oh, come on," Fatma winked at me. "Do you want him now?"

I was not ready to make such a quick decision but I thought that I might not be able to free myself from Dancho the next day. Mother had invited a brilliant family of lawyers to dinner. She was in her second year of studying law and a number of bright constellations from the law universe were always visiting our home. Any barrister or notary was flattered to be her guest, of course.

She had not graduated yet but tributes were sung in her honor noting her particular legal talents. I still cannot explain why she forced me to attend these dinners; my father usually stayed with us for no more than eight minutes—that was the length of time he could endure without cursing—then somebody would call him on his mobile to sign an important business deal.

It was mother who always arranged this, carefully selecting the person who would telephone my father. She chose my attire for the dinners as well. "We'll hide your thighs with this," she would murmur, slipping a black skirt on me; her theory was that the black color concealed the extra fat. Alas, under the black skirt my legs were like mountains of the Himalayas. "And we'll hide your belly with this. Can't you suck your stomach in a little?" she would ask, very concerned; in those moments I hated her. "We must find a dancing partner for you."

Now Fatma, who perhaps was my mother's age but looked three times older with the plaster of makeup on her face and the parallels and meridians under it, repeated her question: "Do you want him now?"

I had to make up my mind.

"I want him now," I answered, meditating no further. "But where will we get to know each other? I can't bring him to my home."

"Your parents will object, eh?" Fatma winked and patted me on the cheek. "Your folks have fed you well, that's why they protect you so much. And they're right. If you don't mind using one of the dresses you bought to spread on the floor, you can get to know him within a minute." Then she scrutinized me from head to toe. "Honey, step out of my shop," her chin pointed at the old cardboard boxes full of rags. "You might steal my merchandise while I'm gone. Wait for me outside. I'll bring the guy in a minute."

"How much will it cost?" I asked her. My father always started any negotiation with the question "How much? US dollars, British pounds or Euros?"

"I want five levs. You can give him … well that's something between him and you. Work it out for yourself."

Fatma took me out into the corridor. People must have been living there for there was a picture of a family on one of the boxes, a father, a mother and three kids, boys whose hair was cropped to the very bone of the skull. I figured they'd had lice. There was purple wallpaper on all the walls with some variation of a horrible flower pattern that had surely brought both parents and children to the edge of insanity. The strips of wallpaper were ripped off and stuck desperately to the floor; the cracked brick masonry covered by thick patches of mold was visible under them.

I thought about the wallpaper in my room, about the marble floor and my bed, which my father had bought for me from Austria. There was a button I could push that would lift it to a certain angle whenever I wanted to sit up; there was another button that made the bed sway like an ocean liner. I had a waterbed as well that mother had bought for me during one of her excursions to North America. I took out one of the dresses that I had acquired; it was dark red, faded and frayed at the hem. Mother wouldn't even have allowed me to throw it into our wastebin for fear it was full of nits, tapeworm, ticks and other vermin. I could spread that dress on the floor, but where? Suddenly I was scared.

What was I doing?

It was summer. My father had made plans to go to Austria and import a new batch of used automobiles; he intended to import two tractors at a very advantageous price. He was a successful international businessman. What was I doing in this narrow walkway? The scorching heat

outside had made the ground split the way men severed
the bones of a slaughtered pig. Even the flagstones of the
sidewalk had become unglued from the sweltering sun, but
the slime in the cellar had not yet dried up. A suspicious
stink reached my nose.

"Men are wicked and envious, love," Fatma had remarked when we entered the room I was to wait in. "They
want to ruin my business, so they throw dead puppies in
the flooded cellar. It's not dangerous. No one from this
block of flats has died yet. Some guys coughed a little on
account of the smell, but then they forgot about it."

After a short time of waiting I heard footsteps along
the flight of stairs that reverberated like slaps in my face.
After several seconds Fatma appeared, her makeup smiling
greasily for it was evident she had plastered another layer
of it and had erased the sweaty streams leading to her
withered breasts.

"Here he comes," she announced, leading by the arm a
mere strip of a man whom she pushed towards me. "He's
very scrawny, it's true," she admitted. "But the guy is tough
and strong, mind you. Every night he unloads marble slabs
at the station in Pernik," she looked at me closely, slapped
my cheek and suddenly snapped, "Spread your dress here
and don't make the bloke wait. I won't let you in the shop,
you might pilfer anything, just anything," then she turned
around, the slaps of her steps echoed down the stairs of
the flooded cellar.

The string-thin streak of a man that unloaded marble
slabs at the station and I were alone. He was much taller

than me, lanky and narrow-shouldered like a shoe box, and his hips were as broad as my upper arm. He was wearing a dirty lilac T-shirt and a pair of jeans that were cut off above the knees, and from there a net of tousled threads hung loosely to the concrete floor. The maypole immediately took off his cut jeans.

His eyes were muddily green, almost yellow; then he took off his dirty T-shirt and flaunted his lusterless puny chest before me. I remembered the men in the pictures of my mother's porno magazines which I had peeked at; their muscles had been taut, bulging like fighter aircraft, while the muscles of the maypole were practically invisible. It was impossible to miss the detail that the man wore nothing under his jeans, and it felt awkward staring at the part of his body that interested me most.

He came toward me and didn't make any efforts to undress me. My blouse had pasted itself with sweat to my paunch. It turned out I was incapable of taking off my skirt, so I let him help me. His efforts were great and futile, which made me doubt that he could actually unload marble if he couldn't manage somebody's backside—even if it was my backside. I took hold of his shoulders, which felt brittle beneath my fingers.

"Say 'I love you,'" I ordered.

"I love you," the guy repeated obediently.

"Say 'You are the only girl I love in the world'," I commanded.

"You are the only... it's too long," the maypole complained and added, "I want ten levs."

"Ok."

"I want them now."

"No. After."

My father's favorite saying was "Don't pay beforehand if you want good service."

I touched him, the place on a man's body I had always dreamt of touching. My hand burned. He groaned. My father's groans were the same: like when a bone gets stuck in a cat's throat and the cat tries to spit it out. It was strange I didn't feel the pain I had read about. It didn't hurt at all; it didn't feel so great either. I simply had to live through it and explore the sensation again. The man's eyes had become purely yellow and shone like crystals of cracked mica on his dark face. He clung to me, a drowning rat clutching at the skin of a whale. It felt as if he were driving nails into a bag of down, rocking slowly, his eyes of mica hidden under shut eyelids.

His narrow shoulders could sink effortlessly into every part of my big body; I myself sank pleasantly downwards into the concrete floor, nurturing a vague idea that I'd bore a hole in it any minute.

Suddenly the man relaxed with his eyes still closed. Saliva ran from his mouth resembling the glitter of the mica I had noticed in his eyes. The guillotine of my buttocks pressed a little pool of blood to the concrete floor, which did not make any impression on me. Theoretically I had been prepared for it. I could already report that in practical terms no matter how fat I was I had become a woman. The sliver forgot to get down from me, yawned, and fell asleep in the comfortable nest of my blubber. Even though he was scrawny, I could feel his weight heavily on me, so I budged and his head hit the floor. The guy was startled, but only for a moment, then yawned again, revealing a lake of saliva shining in his mouth, his dark hands clinging to me, like pencils writing the enormous sentence of my body.

Suddenly the beanpole broke into a sweat and started slithering on to me, and then unexpectedly his lips grounded inaccurately upon mine. I don't know if I could count this as my first kiss with a man, but since I hadn't experienced an event like it before I decided I might as well accept it as such.

This happened when my father was still alive.

I felt overwhelmed with happiness and wanted to get out of there before the happiness melted like everything that came my way, so I shook the guy who slept quietly on top of me and whispered in his ear, "Say 'I love you'." The tone of my voice was the same as my mother's when she talked to the notaries and lawyers, offering them her perfect profile or a glimpse of her pearly leg. I couldn't explain how an intonation like that was born in my throat.

The beanpole did not obey. His yellow eyes hung over my face, his mouth pressing mine. I had some money in the pocket of my blouse. It was very hard to thrust my fingers in the silk pocket glued to my skin. It took several minutes to extract a ten-lev banknote, which I left on the floor saying, "Take it."

"Wait a minute," the man said. His hand, rapid and

scorching like lightening, grabbed the money, then he left me on the dress I had bought from Fatma. At that moment I felt the stink. Fatma was probably right; her neighbors had thrown dead puppies or worse in her cellar.

After five minutes the guy returned carrying two bottles of beer and a package containing the cheapest possible, suspiciously rosy-colored, sausage a man could buy in the cheap shops, squeezed in cellars and bungalows along the Struma River.

He opened one of the bottles, poured half of it down his throat, burped and gave it to me. I tasted a gulp of the liquid and was about to drop dead instantly; the beer smelled no better than the puppies ruining Fatma's business. The man ripped the sausage into two equal pieces, not bothering to peel its skin, tearing it with his teeth as if he hadn't eaten for four years. I felt nauseated watching the beanpole eat the sausage; I suspected I might have to drive him if not to the morgue, then at least to Pirogov Hospital.

"Eat," he said. "I bought the sausage for you."

"And spent all the money," I snapped angrily. He made no comment on my remark, just went on chewing with his mouth open and stuffed with pieces of the cheap sausage soaked in the nasty beer. Then his head dropped to the ridge formed by my breasts. He pushed aside the last piece of sausage and turned again to me.

It felt so good that for a moment I thought, "God bless you, Fatma!" Before I went home I remembered only the guy's scrawny ribs bulging like piano keys in his chest. My mother had had her heart set on making me play the piano and wasted heaps of money on tutors Dancho, my father's loyal chauffeur, would drive directly from the Academy of Classical Music in Sofia to my music room.

I reached almost to the man's dimpled, stubbly chin. He let his hand drop on my head; his fingers felt like my fathers, although some of the nails were crushed and warped. He ran them through my thick, toothbrush-bristles hair and mumbled, "Your hair's red like a bundle of carrots."

My hairstyle resembled a helmet, and mother criticized me severely on that account. How was it possible, she asked rightfully, that a young promising lady would get her hair cut like an infantryman? I was fat, and the hair baking my skull in its red-hot furnace made me feel hotter.

The lanky man's hair was black, dirty, tousled, and covered his shoulders. I didn't ask what his name was.

As I walked down the stairs to the cellar full of bilge water, slime, and pond scum, his steps behind me did not sound like slaps in the face, they reminded me of the first drops of rain after a two-year drought.

"Hey," he shouted. "When will I see you again?"

When? I wouldn't be able to get to this shabby suburb in the near future. All over the district the eight-story flat buildings jutted out from the sidewalks with drab balconies covered by necklaces of drying clothes and linen. Among the blocks, cars, trucks, even several buses were parked and between them stray dogs sauntered, lolling out their tongues, some sprawled like corpses under the buses parked on the asphalt, which melted in the heat.

I didn't think even for a moment that my father would ever allow me to come here. If mother learned that her daughter had been wasting her time in this lair of thugs (let alone the fact that she had visited the building with the flooded cellar and dead dogs!) she would convince my father to buy a house in one of the upscale districts of Sofia, the capital city. I wouldn't be able to see the lanky guy ever again.

"Listen," I told him. "Come to the Snowdrop Cafe tomorrow evening at seven. Then I'll tell you where you can meet me."

There could be no doubt that I would be seeing this man again. There could be no doubt that it had been the most marvelous day of my life. In my chest of drawers I had a lot of money; if I bought a small flat, a flat with one single room and a bathroom—one rotten flat in this swamp of crumbling buildings—then everything would be all right. If I spread an old mattress on the concrete floor I could invite the beanpole and no one would know anything about it. Even Fatma wouldn't. Where could I buy the small one-room flat? It would be best to choose one in the center of town, near the library, for what sort of place could be honored by the visits of Bloody Rayo's daughter but the library?

My father would often remark, "Read, my girl, read. Science was out of my reach, but it will be within yours." My mother paid the best teachers in English, in computers, modern and Latin dances, and good manners to train me. Most recently, she stumbled upon the idea to get a German teacher as well: a spinster with withered cheeks who always visited our home in smashingly expensive shoes. My mother adored her for that—she could adore only expensive things. That was the reason she had been so impressed by the young doctor Xanov who patched up my father after his drunken sprees.

Yes, the only place I was allowed to go was the library. I never visited any fitness clubs; I was too fat, so my father built a gym onto our house and hired a personal trainer to set my targets and measure my progress. But my father, no matter how generous he was, wouldn't be allowed to buy the public library even though he had donated a dozen grand to repair the broken roof tiles. I doubt, however, he was interested in the books for himself, rather his interest in one of the librarians could account for the generosity: a puny woman with the unhappiest eyes that you could imagine, as if someone beat her non-stop around the clock. I wondered why my father liked small women with eyes as sad as death himself. The only exception to this rule was mother who was neither sad nor small, but she left him all the same.

Well, my point is that I had more than enough money to buy a rotten one-room flat. If I did buy it myself, though, the news would spread through town like fire. I had no friends I could trust. The second most beloved saying my father used was "Money is the most loyal friend to man." I could ask a lawyer to acquire the flat for me. If I added two or three rolls of bills to his fee everything could be arranged within twenty-four hours and any lawyer would willingly keep as quiet as the eel in Doctor Xanov's aquarium, an animal my mother often admired.

"Don't you want to do this again?" the lanky youth asked, pushing his dimpled chin into the bristle of my thick short hair.

"I'll tell you tomorrow," I answered. "Seven o'clock at the Snowdrop Cafe. I'll give you more money."

"And we'll buy beer and sausages," he snorted happily.

All this happened before my father was shot, perhaps half a year before his funeral. Neither he nor mother had any inkling about my decision to take money from my drawer.

The apartment was desperately small. An empty room in a block of old flats, with its window facing north, a roof made of worm-eaten logs, crumbling plaster on the ceiling, a small empty kitchen, and a bathroom so tiny that I had to enter with my shoulder first to relieve myself. There was electricity, but unfortunately there was neither hot water nor any heat whatsoever. I bought a mattress and a cheap blanket, then I invited the maypole whose name I still didn't know.

The room was as narrow as a coffin; the lawyer was so curious about why I wanted it so badly that I had to lie to him. I told him that I intended to house my German tutor there. The lawyer smiled, which, according to the code of judicial behavior, meant, "Bloody Rayo's fat cow has a screw loose, no doubt about it. Her father has stuffed her so full of money that it's interfering with her brain Well, I didn't give a damn about his inferences.

I became the owner of the room with the mattress in less than twenty-four hours. This event once again confirmed my father's thesis that money would do more for you than your best friend. I didn't have any friends.

Before the battered entrance door banged shut behind his back the beanpole had taken off his jeans and his dirty lilac T-shirt, the same one as before. And, like before, he did not have any underwear on.

"What's your name?" I asked him.

"Simo," he said.

"Don't you want to know what my name is?" It was evident he didn't and so he clung to me instead, a thin rope spiraling about the masts of my endless buttocks. "Aren't you interested in what my name is?" He didn't answer, and couldn't possibly do so because his mouth was full of saliva that shined in the light like mica. My mother had a diamond necklace that shined like that—and a diamond ring, and there was a diamond on the belt of her formal evening dress. My father had brought it to her from Austria. So I decided that the saliva in his mouth wasn't mica; it was diamond. "OK. My name is Moni. Did you hear me? Moni. Here's the money. Take it."

He didn't look at the money because his body had already started swinging over me. I pushed him aside, which wasn't difficult at all. He banged against the floor but his reaction surprised me.

"You're pretty," he said. "You are pretty."

It was at that moment that I understood how the other women felt: my mother; my classmates in the private school for girls, my tutors in English, German, modern dances, fitness and good manners. The other women whose boyfriends told them they were pretty, that they weren't fat bulldozers but simply pretty women.

"You are off your rocker," I objected, but he didn't hear me.

On the fortieth day after my father's funeral mother paid for a solemn church service and invited all the intellectuals and financial elite of the town. Or, I should say, all the people that mother considered elite. The church service was an excellent opportunity for her to show off her mourning attire. On such occasions (and by "such occasions" I'm referring to opportunities for my mother to show off) she always hired the cook from "Casablanca," the most expensive and posh restaurant in Pernik.

All were enchanted by the menu she offered and by her fashion. I was already very familiar with the cook's menus because mother abided by her sacred law once a week, on Friday, to take me out to dinner to "Casablanca." I had the feeling that the waiter knew when we were about to arrive by the sound of my mother's jeep. The same very tall and attractive man always met us at the door, taking my mother's hat or cape and bowing gracefully, down to the last vertebra in his spinal cord, and whispering very sincerely, "You look just wonderful, Madam!"

The words would rattle like pebbles in his mouth, his eyes following my mother with such demonstrative admiration that I suspected he was ready to kiss the pavement beneath her shoes; it was hardly surprising when she would leave him fabulous tips.

Then the waiter would take my hat or coat and bring the menu, his eyes shining proudly for he had again anticipated what my mother would order. "Shall it be shark's loin prepared in the Saragossa way, Madame?" My mother made it a special point for all her guests to be aware of the fact she ate shark's loin in the Saragossa way.

She had grown up in a family of waiters. My grandmother and grandfather, her parents, experts in this trade, had nurtured several generations of drunkards at "The White Elephant" restaurant, and after the establishment went bankrupt they set up a pub in one of the most backwater suburbs of the town. My grandmother Shar (I suppose it was probably an abbreviation of "shark") was slim and still had her sharp green eyes even though she was getting on in years. Compared to her my grandfather resembled an obituary notice. He made cheap cocktails behind the bar but more often drank quietly and sadly with his regular customers, not giving a damn about the rest of the world. His only daughter, my mother, had money to burn and therefore was happy. Grandfather was given to noble charity, ordering free drinks for his old friends, a bunch of poor pensioners with receding hair who poured the cheap cocktails into their brains, blessing him day and night.

Grandma Shar looked at them with disdain, burning them with the green flames of her eyes. In her rare fits of wrath she would throw my grandpa's friends out of the establishment in a most ignominious manner, but this happened once in a blue moon so they waited for death peacefully, full to the brim with brandy my grandfather sold to them cheap, for although my grandfather was a drunkard with thinning hair, he never swindled his old pals.

As my mother entertained her guests, barely remembering the reason for the occasion, I was wondering if it was a good idea to introduce Simo to my grandfather.

BLOOD OF A MOLE

Few customers visit my shop. They watch the animals in the cages and seldom buy them. The room is narrow and there is no place for me behind the counter, so I usually sit on my old moth-eaten chair behind the door. Hours I stare at frogs, lizards, snakes and insects. Teachers come and take frogs for their biology lessons; fishermen drop in to buy some kind of bait; that is practically all. Soon, I'll have to close my shop and I'll be sorry about it, for the sleepy, gloomy smell of formalin has always given me peace and an odd feeling of home. I have worked here for five years now.

One day a strange small woman entered my room. Her face looked frightened and grey. She approached me, her arms trembling, unnaturally pale, resembling two dead white fish in the dark. The woman did not look at me, nor did she say anything. Her elbows reeled, searching for support on the wooden counter. It seemed she had not come to buy lizards and snails; perhaps she had simply felt unwell and looked for help at the first open door she happened to notice. I was afraid she would fall and took her by the hand. She remained silent and rubbed her lips with a handkerchief. I was at a loss, it was very quiet and dark in the shop.

"Have you moles here?" she suddenly asked. Then I saw her eyes. They resembled old, torn cobwebs with a little spider in the center, the pupil.

"Moles?" I muttered. I had to tell her I never had sold moles in the shop and I had never seen one in my life. The woman wanted to hear something else—an affirmation. I knew it by her eyes, by the timid stir of her fingers that reached out to touch me. I felt uneasy staring at her.

"I have no moles," I said. She turned to go, silent and crushed, her head drooping between her shoulders. Her steps were short and uncertain.

"Hey, wait!" I shouted. "Maybe I have some moles." I don't know why I acted like this.

Her body jerked, there was pain in her eyes. I felt bad because I couldn't help her.

"The blood of a mole can cure sick people," she whispered. "You only have to drink three drops of it."

I was scared. I could feel something evil lurking in the dark.

"It eases the pain at least," she went on dreamily, her voice thinning into a sob.

"Are you ill?" I asked. The words whizzed by like a shot in the thick moist air and made her body shake. "I'm sorry."

"My son is ill."

Her transparent eyelids hid the faint, desperate glitter of her glance. Her hands lay numb on the counter, lifeless like firewood. Her narrow shoulders looked narrower in her frayed grey coat.

"A glass of water will make you feel better," I said.

She remained motionless and when her fingers grabbed the glass her eyelids were still closed. She turned to go, small and frail, her back hunching, her steps noiseless and impotent in the dark. I ran after her. I had made up my mind.

"I'll give you blood of a mole!" I shouted.

The woman stopped in her tracks and covered her face with her hands. It was unbearable to look at her. I felt empty. The eyes of the lizards sparkled like pieces of broken glass. I didn't have any mole's blood. I didn't have any moles. I imagined the woman in the room, sobbing. Perhaps she was still holding her face with her hands. Well, I closed the door so that she could not see me, then I cut my left wrist with a knife. The wound bled and slowly oozed into a little glass bottle. After ten drops had covered the bottom, I ran back to the room where the woman was waiting for me.

"Here it is," I said. "Here's the blood of a mole."

She didn't say anything, just stared at my left wrist. The wound still bled slightly, so I thrust my arm under my apron. The woman glanced at me and kept silent. She did not reach for the glass bottle, rather she turned and hurried toward the door. I overtook her and forced the bottle into her hands.

"It's blood of a mole!"

She fingered the transparent bottle. The blood inside sparkled like dying fire. Then she took some money out of her pocket.

"No. No," I said.

Her head hung low. She threw the money on the

counter and did not say a word. I wanted to accompany her to the corner. I even poured another glass of water, but she would not wait. The shop was empty again and the eyes of the lizards glittered like wet pieces of broken glass.

Cold, uneventful days slipped by. The autumn leaves whirled hopelessly in the wind, giving the air a brown appearance. The early winter blizzards hurled snowflakes against the windows and sang in my veins. I could not forget that woman. I'd lied to her. No one entered my shop and in the quiet dusk I tried to imagine what her son looked like. The ground was frozen, the streets were deserted and the winter tied its icy knot around houses, souls and rocks.

One morning, the door of my shop opened abruptly. The same small grey woman entered and before I had time to greet her, she rushed and embraced me. Her shoulders were weightless and frail, and tears were streaking her delicately wrinkled cheeks. Her whole body shook and I thought she would collapse, so I caught her trembling arms. Then the woman grabbed my left hand and lifted it up to her eyes. The scar of the wound had vanished but she found the place. Her lips kissed my wrist, her tears made my skin warm. Suddenly it felt cosy and quiet in the shop.

"He walks!" The woman sobbed, hiding a tearful smile behind her palms. "He walks!"

She wanted to give me money; her big black bag was full of different things that she had brought for me. I could feel the woman had braced herself up, her fingers had become tough and stubborn. I accompanied her to the corner but she only stayed there beside the street-lamp, looking at me, small and smiling in the cold.

It was so cosy in my dark shop and the old, imperceptible smell of formalin made me dizzy with happiness. My lizards were so beautiful that I loved them as if they were my children.

In the afternoon of the same day, a strange man entered my room. He was tall, scraggly and frightened.

"Have you... the blood of a mole?" he asked, his eyes piercing through me. I was scared.

"No, I haven't. I have never sold moles here."

"Oh, you have! You have! Three drops... three drops, no more... My wife will die. You have! Please!"

He squeezed my arm.

"Please... three drops! Or she'll die..."

My blood trickled slowly from the wound. The man held a little bottle and the red drops gleamed in it like embers. Then the man left and a little bundle of bank-notes rolled on the counter.

On the following morning a great whispering mob of strangers waited for me in front of my door. Their hands clutched little glass bottles.

"Blood of a mole! Blood of a mole!"

They shouted, shrieked, and pushed each other. Everyone had a sick person at home and a knife in his hand.

THE OLD HOUSE

Ena's grandfather Goran built the house sixty years ago. He was a powerful merchant and traded in wheat, medicines, cotton and wool, which he exported to Romania. He had made heaps of money even before the cholera epidemics struck. In the troubled times during World War II, he took to his heels, hid in Romania and fell in love with a Romanian woman there. He dumped Ena's grandmother, Mladena, and the woman pined away slowly, alone in the unfinished house. He had built the roof above the rooms, true, but there were no doors or windows, and the brick walls had not been plastered. Goran and Mladena had no children. That was the main reason why he took all the money and beat it to Austria, or perhaps to Italy with that Romanian beauty. He badly wanted an heir, he had often said. The Romanian woman, in Mladena's opinion, was by no means pretty, just a prattling Gypsy who made eyes at her husband.

Grandma Mladena found herself broke. She came into possession of two wardrobes of fine Austrian suits, two suitcases stuffed with dresses, and a house with a dozen spacious rooms with high ceilings which in winter froze with cold that no stove in the world could drive away. The neglected wife hung her head in shame. She became the

42

talk of the town and, having no official documents, she couldn't sell the enormous building: actually, not a building but several dozen gaping walls.

Mladena tried to sell her dresses. Nobody wanted a barren woman's clothes – your daughter wouldn't conceive and the whole town would jabber about that. Then Mladena started selling her husband's suits. She attracted a few customers: Goran was a big shot in these parts, and his name was as good as gold in your purse. Mladena hoped that a brick-layer or a plasterer would buy her husband's Austrian jackets. She put a sheet of paper on the front door: **"I sell half-price suits to plasterers."** But you would find no plasterers in that town, where people made their houses of wattle and daub. Finally a man came to see the Austrian garments.

"I am a plasterer," he said. "Give me one of these half-price suits."

"If you really are a plasterer I'd like you to put plaster on the walls and ceilings of my house," she said. "I'll let you live in the cellar or in that small room over there. But you'll have to plaster the kitchen first. I'll cook for you. You appear to be poor. I will sell Goran's household goods and I'll pay you."

That plasterer gave Mladena the once-over and said, "Your neighbors told me your husband dumped you because you couldn't have a child. Listen, I'm looking for a woman exactly like you. I won't squander money on tarts while I plaster your house. Do I make myself clear? We'll live together, you'll cook for me and you'll wash my clothes.

I'll plaster the walls and I'll put in windows, too. If you agree, let's do it. If I like you, I'll start plastering right away."

Mladena said, "But there's not even a bed here."

"So? The floor will do. Don't waste my time. If I don't like you, I'll leave five leva. I never leave a woman more than a fiver. If I like you, I'll plaster the kitchen."

He left her a fiver and made himself scarce, but after a week he came again and took to plastering. The man gave up after a couple of days, left another fiver on the kitchen floor and decamped from the house, dressed in one of Goran's suits, a pair of Goran's sandals on his feet. After a month he came back, but Goran's suit and Goran's sandals were gone. The man wore shorts, even though this June was cold. He'd lost his garments gambling, he said. Then Rafko, that was his name, got down to plastering again – but he often needed Mladena's help. He told her she'd better spread a blanket on the floor "every now and then," and he'd leave a fiver for her. The problem was he had no money, but she could calculate how much he owed her. Rafko ate up all the bread and cheese in the house, and there were no potatoes or turnips in the cellar. Mladena didn't have a penny to bless herself with. She had already sold Goran's suits, Goran's shoes, Goran's chairs and Goran's cupboards, so she really counted on the thirty-seven fivers the plasterer owed her. The only thing she hadn't sold was a sewing machine; she planned to pawn it. If worse came to worst, she intended to pull down the house and sell the bricks. She hoped to live off the bricks until she found a widower with little children. The woman reckoned she could take care of the kids and eke out a living with their father.

One day, Mladena grew desperate and put another advertisement on a piece of cardboard, "**I sell half-price SINGER sewing machine to a widower with little children.**"

Meanwhile Rafko plodded along, plastering the living room, but his trowel left humpbacked or cracked walls in its wake. When there was no more food in the kitchen, he stole potatoes and onions from other gardens, or he gambled - Mladena couldn't tell for sure. Sometimes in the evening, he brought loads of food in black plastic sacks: muddy potatoes lay on top of loaves of bread, occasional chocolates, or sausages; you could find all that in Rafko's roomy bags. He gorged himself on peppers, olives, and cookies thrust into his mouth all at once. The more he ate the less he plastered, spending most of his time with Mladena on her only blanket. One day he suggested, "Listen, I'd better stop paying you. I've already fallen into your ways. You are as meek as a ewe. I'll plaster your house for free and instead of living in the cellar I'll move in with you. I'll treat Priest Mano to a glass of brandy; he'd marry us for free. We won't go to the church. He'll marry us in front of the SINGER, do you agree? Then I can go when I am fed up with you, and God won't be cross with me."

He lied to Mladena. He didn't treat Priest Mano to a glass of brandy; he borrowed twenty leva from him instead. Rafko said he wanted to buy a wedding ring for his bride. He lied again, of course. He bought a tuxedo, a tie and a bed. A German engineer fell ill and soon met his maker. The plasterer took the tux and the tie from the man's body for three leva—dirt cheap indeed—then stowed away the bed the engineer had died in. Rafko promised the German widow to dig a grave for her husband in return for the bed. Of course, no one ever saw that grave.

Actually, Priest Mano couldn't finish the marriage ceremony. Halfway through it the plasterer said, "Stop. That's enough. I don't have money enough for more. Don't make a face at me, Priest Mano. It gets on my nerves! If you make a face again, I'll strip your cassock and sell it to buy Mladena a wedding ring. Do you get my meaning?"

The priest raised hell but Rafko the plasterer clutched him by the throat and started taking off the black cassock. At a certain point, he said, "Actually, nobody would buy your smelly coat, anyway," so he kicked the priest's ass and rushed home to his wife, who had already spread the blanket on the dead German's bed.

Soon, there was no more bread in house again, but Rafko didn't mind.

"For the first time in my life I don't have to pay a woman," he sighed happily, smiling at the gray, still unplastered walls. Rafko sold the SINGER sewing machine and bought three bags of flour, onions and potatoes. He wanted Mladena all the time. After a week, the flour was gone, but he said potatoes would do.

"We have to repair the house," Mladena remembered.

"Take it easy, woman," he roared. "Some time or other I'll plaster the house, to hell with it! Mladena, you are here now, let's grasp this opportunity. Think about me! If you die, what shall I do? I have to search for another woman. Do you think I can find a meek one like you? Not even if I wore out ten pairs of boots looking for her."

"Hey, Rafko," Mladena said one day. "My period is late. Maybe I'll have a baby."

"So what?" he said. "You are not dead yet, are you? Let's seize this opportunity! Don't even think of going out, woman. Well, I'd prefer it if you were barren. But you look pretty to me. If the baby is pretty and healthy, we can sell it for fifty leva to some childless couple."

When Mladena gave birth to a baby girl the townspeople exclaimed, "Wow! That Mladena wasn't barren at all!"

The Romanian beauty Goran had eloped with returned to Bulgaria, found Mladena and said, "Listen, Goran— may worms feast on his liver!—kicked me out because I couldn't have a baby. But you have to know, Mladena, it's all his fault. His seed is no good. It's rotten. Look at you—you gave birth to a baby as big as a calf. I have no roof over my head, Mladena, I'm flat broke. Will you let live in your house with you? You and I will plaster the walls together."

The walls again remained unplastered: Rafko liked the Romanian beauty, kissed her and made her sell first her dress, then her bracelet. After that she pawned her shoes and the two of them drank and sang a couple of weeks in the cellar. Finally Rafko moved in with her "for good." Everything between them was okay while there was bread and cheese in Rafko's bags. The beauty started shouting dirty words in Romanian at him. Once she tied him to the bed, where he had fallen asleep, and thrashed him with his own belt, repeating, "Give me the 96 fivers you owe me!"

The next day, Rafko threw the beauty out into the street with only her nightgown on, poor soul. Then he went to his wife's room, took his baby girl in his hands and started to sing to it. That was one thing the plasterer was good at: God had blessed him with a beautiful voice. The roosters stopped crowing while he sang to the baby in the morning, and the rooks didn't caw in the poplar trees when he crooned a lullaby to her at night. Rafko soon tired of the baby, though, and took off again. After a month or so, he came back to Mladena.

"I can live only with you. You are an angel. An archangel even, and know it." He bowed down before her and kissed her knees. "The Romanian vixen tried to cut my throat twice. She gave me rat poison, too, and I puked up my dinner. She burnt all my underwear. Nasty virago! But you are an angel! Yes, you are, Mladena!" he whispered and kissed her knees once more.

Then Rafko started plastering the walls again, but not with much success. His eyes were on Mladena all the time. He often got down from the scaffolding and said to her, "Hang around me just in case. We can take advantage of the opportunity, you know." From time to time he told her she was an angel, and in the evenings he sang to the baby. He held the little girl, smiled and said, "What a pretty child! She's Daddy's little beauty!"

Then Rafko took to singing and dancing at weddings and at birthday parties. At the end of the day, he brought bags of broiled chickens or pork chops, cheese and some-times even a bundle of five-leva banknotes. Mladena couldn't tell for sure if he'd stolen it all. He bought the baby expensive clothes and never said another word about selling her to a childless couple.

Rafko again vanished into thin air and the neighbors hinted to Mladena that Rafko had eloped to Sofia with a young ballerina. The ceilings and walls of the house re-mained bare, but now there were windows and doors eve-rywhere. Mladena regularly cleaned a wealthy man's stables and washed his wife's clothes. Although people in Pernik were as sensitive as paving stones, once in a blue moon they gave her old clothes for her baby girl. Actually, Mladena had already found her feet when Goran came back home. He looked wealthier than ever, arriving in a dazzling German car. Goran got out of it and saw Mladena's daughter crawling on the front lawn.

"I know what you did while I was away," Goran said to his wife. "It's okay. I'll take you back with the kid."

Perhaps he knew his seed was no good and he could beget nothing but fat bundles and bank accounts. He hired bricklayers, master masons and plasterers; he had the place surrounded with stone walls and nailed gold and silver Austrian rattles above the toddler's cot.

One day while Goran was at work, Rafko the plasterer came back to the town, and lo and behold! He couldn't believe his eyes: Mladena's place was surrounded with a wall, her house was roofed with marble slabs, and the walls looked as if fresh snowflakes had fallen on them an hour ago! He made up his mind to go in and check out what had happened, but at the moment he touched the front door two mutts as big as donkeys descended on him, growling and snarling. "Their throats are deep as caves," Rafko thought, but caves or no caves he went for it. Mladena came out to see what the commotion was. He saw her, jumped eagerly, and shouted, "Let me kiss your knees! You are an angel! An archangel! I wore out twenty pairs of boots looking for a woman like you. Wow! There's no other like you! Take my word for it. Listen, I've got a bag of bread and cheese here. Find a blanket quickly. I can't wait, woman."

"My husband's coming home from work," Mladena said. "He whitewashed the house and put new doors and windows."

"What husband?" Rafko seethed. "Didn't Priest Mano marry us? And whose ass did I kick so he'd get lost and I could kiss you? Mladena, didn't you tell me 'With this ring I thee wed'?"

"But I didn't have a ring," Mladena said.

"So what? Who is the father of the kid in the yard, eh?"

"I tell you: Goran is here," Mladena said. "Go away or he'll shoot you dead."

"We'll see about that!" Rifko said.

Then he tossed some bones to the mutts, hugged the toddler to him and started to sing. A voice as beautiful as the sun poured out of his lips. Mladena forgot that he had sold her SINGER sowing machine, ignored the fact he had left her in the lurch with the baby. She forgot she'd had to clean cow dung all winter. She just listened to Rafko's song. The baby listened, too.

"Come on," Rafko told her. "You know what we're going to do."

"No way," Mladena said. "We can't do that. Goran is coming home. Take the money and go," she said and gave him a roll of banknotes. After Goran returned, there was money stored in all drawers in the kitchen.

"Listen, come here and forget about the money. If by chance you die, then what! You are all right now, so let's take this opportunity."

They didn't stop taking this opportunity until night fell. Then Mladena fed her daughter and Rafko sang to her. He sang and sang as if he had the music of ten hearts in his chest. Goran worked long hours that day. When finally he came home, Rafko and Mladena were about to take the opportunity again, celebrating the fact Mladena was alive. Rafko was saying "There's no other like you!" when he was aware something had gone wrong. A gun was pressed to the back of his skull.

"What are you doing here?" Goran roared.

"Can't you see what I'm doing?" Rafko retorted. "Are you blind? Listen, either kill me with that gun or let me get back to my business!"

Goran flew into a rage and shot. Fortunately for Rafko, he had aimed at the ceiling.

"I sang to the child," Rafko shouted. "I made a family for you. Now you have a daughter to leave your money to, you idiot."

Goran shot once again. His bodyguards rushed into the room like hounds. The next day the neighbors found pools of Rafko's blood and wisps of his brown hair all along the street near Goran's house.

"Put on your clothes," Goran ordered Mladena that night. "If I catch you again with him…see this?" He showed her the big kitchen knife. "I'll cut your throat with it. You know I slaughter cows and lambs, so be careful."

Mladena looked at the marble slabs on the floor.

"Will you throw me out?" she asked.

"Yes," he said.

He didn't throw her out, though. He hired a neighbor to feed and lull the baby to sleep and took Mladena to the cellar where he kept Rafko's tuxedo and tie, the ones that had belonged to the dead German engineer.

"Did that schmuck sing to you?" Goran asked his wife.

"Yes, he did," Mladena said.

"Then I'll sing to you, too," Goran declared. He opened his mouth and thundered out a couple of words. Mladena thought she heard five oxen moo, a bulldog snarl and fireworks splutter. The rooks flew away from the poplar trees, terrified; the roosters crowed even though it was past midnight, and the baby wailed bitterly.

"Does he sing better than me?" Goran asked.

"Yes, he does," Mladena answered.

"But he dumped you!" Goran shouted.

"You dumped me before he did," Mladena said.

Goran took out a fat wad, laid the banknotes on her pillow and said, "He didn't have this! You cleaned cow dung and washed dirty underpants!"

"He kissed my knees," Mladena said.

"Well, I won't kiss your knees," Goran said and put on the tuxedo and the tie.

"Did he look better than me?" Goran asked his wife.

"Yes, he did," Mladena said.

The Romanian beauty came to beg money from Goran, but he set the dogs on her, then took the rifle from the wall to shoot at her. Fortunately for the Romanian, Mladena was there. She gave her bread and some ten-leva bills in an old purse.

"You are a good woman," the beauty said and kissed Mladena's cheeks. "Listen, Goran's bodyguards broke Rafko's legs. Now he's in Sofia and he's a beggar. Give me some more money. I'll find him and I'll help him."

Mladena gave her more ten-leva bills.

Mladena's daughter was very pretty from an early age. Crowds of boys thronged to see her and tell her she was the most beautiful girl they had ever seen. The stone wall that surrounded Goran's house was covered with flowers. Young men wrote on it **"I love you"** in their own blood. Goran looked at the girl, sighed happily and could not believe his eyes. Young men trampled the grass around his house and trod dozens of paths to her window. She was the queen of the town and every day chose another young man, usually the one who brought her the most expensive necklace.

At seventeen, Goran's pretty adopted daughter gave birth to a baby girl, Ena by name. She couldn't tell who the father was—he might have been anyone. Then Rafko's daughter left the baby with Grandma Mladena and Grandpa Goran and went to live in Sofia.

By that time, grandpa Goran was not a rich merchant any more. He was an old man who suffered from rheumatism, and the bones in his body felt like a mouthful of bad teeth. Goran often played chess with another old man, Grandpa Rafko, lame in the left leg. In the evenings, the two geezers drank brandy together, and when the night was warm, the one with the lame leg sang in a beautiful voice. Mladena thought he still had the power and the music of ten hearts in his chest. Grandpa Goran, although his rheumatism tortured him, sang too. In fact, he roared, and wailed, and sputtered as if he had an excavator in his throat, trying to dig a ditch in the street. Mladena thought Goran wanted to frighten her away from the room where the two of them got drunk. However, Grandma Mladena didn't scare easily. She sat opposite the two men, even though she was sleepy and her legs hurt: every square inch of them hurt, but she cooked for the men and poured brandy into their glasses. Sometimes she watched a silly TV show for a change.

Young Ena was a quiet child, beloved by all who knew her: Grandpa Rafko with his angelic voice, Grandpa Goran and Grandma Mladena. The three of them were always by Ena's side, and the baby never wailed or sobbed. She grew up a most tractable child—quieter than the roof tiles, more tranquil than the air in the cellar where no one lived. The four of them lived in the same old house that summers filled with youth and winters with the most beautiful silver one could dream of.

In the evening, her dog waited at the front door. His name was Rain, and his steps sounded like raindrops rolling down a windowpane after midnight. François thought he remained in that town because of the animal. If he went away Rain would starve. Anna forgot to feed him and didn't give him baths. She worked day and night on her short stories and translations. Oceans of love roared in the books she translated into French. There was no food at home. She stared at her computer like a bat, her hair disheveled, her dictionaries scattered under the table, on the floor, in the corridor.

Rain lay in the corner on his tattered pillow and looked at her. She swore at the long sentences and drank constantly: milk from a bottle or strong black beer that made her eyes glisten like those of a sick man. She ignored that François had come home. She poured milk into a saucer for Rain. The dog smelled it, and it was suddenly warm in her eyes. Sometimes she gave Rain beer too, and he snarled, his teeth shining, wild and sharp.

François went to the kitchen and made sandwiches for her. There were dirty dishes in the sink, and her shoes and stockings were all over the corridor. She wore socks of different colors and she had put on one of his sweatshirts, the first one she stumbled across. Sometimes she wore his leather jacket, too.

That day she had not aired the room, and at noon the curtains were drawn. Although the window was not that big, François loved to look out of it. He watched the warehouse full of ramshackle used cars and felt some of the tension fall out of his body. She translated her books and breathed the stale air. This time she didn't even look up. When he brought her sandwiches, she wolfed them down and forgot about him almost right away. François went to sleep, imagining she mumbled something under her breath.

Rain had got accustomed to her voice and waited by her side, staring at her dictionaries and at her old computer. François slept on the mattress around which CDs, sheets of paper and her books were scattered. Well after midnight, half-awake, he felt her lying beside him. She didn't wait for him to drift out of sleep. She kissed him savagely as if to punish him. She loved him without saying a word then suddenly called him names as bad as November downpours. François couldn't live like that any more. He couldn't bear the stale air that waited for him every night. He hated her dog and her love. It was a moment of sunshine that slipped behind a cloud, leaving him starving in the fog of Brussels.

He had tried to go away several times, but Rain followed him, his steps like raindrops hitting the pavement. François feared that one day the dog would die among the dictionaries and the characters in her short stories. Several times Rain had run after him behind the puddle that surrounded the warehouse, behind the used cars where Anna went to draw inspiration from the cold, moist air. She was a poor eater. Her face became paler and more impenetrable as she wandered among the used cars. The dog brought autumn in its wake, it almost always started to drizzle when Rain went out.

François suspected that if he left that place, Anna wouldn't come back to that window to the north, and the light of her computer would burn all the characters she had invented.

There wouldn't be anyone there to open the window and get rid of the heavy air—riddled with idioms—that she adored. François was sick and tired of her silly love. She slept atop his chest, her skin as thin as the wind. Rain watched them, quiet, more and more miserable, his fur thin and falling off with old age.

One day François left for good. Rain followed him, his eyes glowing in the mist. Even after François caught the bus the dog ran after him, his fur dirty and shabby, a scrawny old thing that brought the autumn fog and left it to live above the spire of the quiet church Notre Dame d'Evere. Anna had told him that winters began and ended in Notre Dame d'Evere. He loved the quiet short January afternoons that were born in the streets around the church. François would be sorry if a truck driver or a motorcyclist ran over the dog. The animal had sensed that this was the day François would leave. That day, Rain ran after the bus to the railway station. François jumped onto the first train on Platform 1 headed for Oostende, the noisy Belgian port he had never liked. The dog gave a howl and dashed after the train, but soon lost the game and collapsed on the rails, frail and miserable in his thinning fur. François heaved a sigh of relief when the train pushed its way into the tunnel and Rain disappeared from sight, his howl dissolving in the rain. I hope he wasn't run over by a train, François thought.

Later he often tried to drive away the thought of that cold room, of the window onto the rows of used cars and the big black puddle around the warehouse. He saw her computer that spewed out words in the night, and hated to think that now there was no one to make sandwiches for her.

Many times he felt like running back to the house. François was glad he lived in a big noisy town far away from her short stories. Monotonous West-Vlaanderen, the cars on the speedways, the winter and the tunnels separated him from her dictionaries. François hated the bridges, which led to her street. He tried to blot out the memories of that place, so he bought a dog and called him Rain, too, but his bull terrier didn't have autumns and peaceful fog in his eyes, and didn't look shabby the way her dog did.

François sometimes wondered what had happened to her, but he had no more life to waste. Of course he found another girl who was sparklingly clean and healthy. She loved him and she didn't make him think of old computers, black puddles and rows of used cars. It was odd that once in a while he could hear quiet raindrops in his dreams, very odd.

In early summer he crossed the West-Vlaanderen that stretched between him and the rows of old used automobiles. He didn't go on business; he even didn't want to meet Anna. Perhaps at the back of his mind he hoped he might glimpse her, nothing more.

That day François got out of the taxi, calm and reserved. He had a good job in Oostende, he made a lot of money. He hoped he had forgotten the shabby and deserted street. No way. He knew every inch of it.

He felt like running to her building but had a drink instead. A glass of brandy always helped him. The speedway and the cars had gone, and there were no tunnels either. The house waited and the puddle was there, big and black like autumn. Suddenly he heard raindrops behind his back. It was raining, it was raining indeed! There were no peaceful afternoons and silver rains in the town on the Nordsee where he lived. There were clean carpets, brand new electrical appliances, neatly arranged books and pictures in his house. There wasn't a single dictionary there. He had told his wife that, years ago, he knew a girl, a translator, and he had spoken about the characters in her short stories. His wife threw all dictionaries out of their home. She loved him and looked after him very well.

He noticed a vague silhouette. A woman appeared. She was so thin and pale that François could not breathe. The warehouse was silent. Suddenly it stopped raining. She was the most beautiful girl he had ever seen.

He suddenly thought of his clean house with the carpets and books and pictures on the walls. He thought of the train that would take him home. He had crossed West-Vlaanderen to speak to the building she lived in.

François could hear the raindrops fall. He couldn't move

and he knew something had broken inside him. The vast plains of West-Vlaanderen had not helped. The brandy hadn't either. The tunnels were all gone. He turned around. A dog, scraggy and weak, trailed after him. The man felt like shouting. The dog's fur was shabby and miserable, but he loved it. The dog, whose steps were raindrops, stood still and watched him. There were silver Brussels afternoons in his eyes. They sparkled with joy, they were happy François had come back. Many autumns and winters François had loved that dog.

"Rain, Rain!" François whispered.

The dog trembled, approached him and let him touch his shabby back.

"How's Anna?" François asked.

HUMBOLDT STREET

Their evenings together were short and beautiful. Ivonne liked the little Bavarian restaurant at the very end of Humboldt Strasse, and she liked the quiet clean room on the second floor above the restaurant where Dietrich took her. She loved the rain outside the windows. It had a gentle impatience Dietrich didn't have for her. It soothed her. There was no winter and no summer there, in that Humbodt Street. There was drizzle and there were lawns, and there were always clouds the color of cold tea that reassured her. The first time Dietrich brought her to Humboldt Street she felt miserable. He didn't speak or smile while she told him about her job in the translation pool. Then things changed. She learned to love his silences. Dietrich was quiet and very clean. He listened to her, it rained, and the whole town of Monchengladbach waited behind her closed eyes. It was pleasant to have Dietrich's sweetly scented skin by her side. She liked his shadow. She liked his shirts and his long thin fingers. She liked his gray eyes and his *"Bis spaeter!"* which didn't mean "See you soon." It meant "See you next Friday."

Their evenings together happened on Fridays, then they happened on Tuesdays and Fridays, too, even on Mondays, the evening and Dietrich's silences a promise in the fresh wind, their clean room on the second floor an island of quiet. Ivonne's life was an autumn of endless November but it was a happy November with Dietrich's beautiful hands and beautiful smell that lingered in her mind long after he was gone. She felt she had to protect him from his gloom. She loved him eagerly and tactfully, she kissed him patiently, gently, then angrily and rudely because he was so inert and silent. She learned to like his quiet immobility; it was warm and unobtrusive like a windless day. She enjoyed every inch of his quiet skin, a pale continent her kisses had mapped with patient precision.

Their evenings together happened in the morning, too, when he telephoned they needed to talk. He said "*Ich moechte mit dir sprechen*," "I'd like to have a word with you." Her steps to him were their conversation, his beautiful shadow waiting for her to love it. There was no end waiting for Dietrich. He didn't tell her where he worked or if he worked at all, the room on the second floor was enough for her November. He left her a ring once, and he left her another one the next time. He didn't say he was happy to see her and didn't tell her she was magnificent. It felt that way, though. When on Sundays there was no "*Ich moechte mit dir sprechen*," she hated her apartment. The quiet in it was bad for the translations she worked on, her anxiety killed the metaphors and the month of November ended. She tried to forget about Humboldt Street. She couldn't work. She had to go out.

She strolled along Nopius Strasse and drank a beer at Kleiner Weinkeller, a cheap cozy pub that smelled of sweet beer and weak wine. Her life was a cozy pub. She knew its customers were long gone home and the old counter shimmered empty, warm and dry in the night. She liked it that way. At Kleiner Weinkeller, she drank her beer sitting next to Hans- Jurgen, another quiet man who didn't pay attention to her when she said "Hi" from across the bar. He was a computer programmer. He was almost as tall and as quiet as Dietrich and he didn't mind listening to Ivonne speaking about her translations. His skin didn't feel soft and translucent the way Dietrich's did and it had no odor. One man simply replaced another in Ivonne's month of November, in the rain that quietly mixed with the night. Neither Dietrich nor Hans-Jurgen had told her she made a difference.

A month or two ago—Ivonne couldn't be sure when exactly that happened—she had been obsessed with a long abstract poem that sounded colder than the sky—Hans-Jurgen Mark gave her a wedding ring. It was cheap and poorly made, not even silver. Hans-Jurgen had said, "Next Sunday I'll marry you."

It was raining hard next Sunday. Ivonne had not translated the poem to the end. The old pub where Hans-Jurgen was supposed to wait for her was closed. Hans-Jurgen didn't show up—he wasn't in front of the church Jacob Kirche, or in "The Green Lemon" restaurant where they'd planned to eat an expensive lunch. She didn't know where to look for him, so that Sunday she didn't marry anybody. She tried to translate that difficult poem instead. She went to another good pub, "The Steigbuegel Pub," which meant "The Stirrup."

"*Ich moechte mit dir sprechen,,*" a man said to her. Dietrich. She had not expected to find him there.

His new car looked expensive and when she asked him how much it cost, he answered, "It's nothing. I own flats, which I rent."

That day, Dietrich was calm and she read her new translations to him. He didn't say a word of praise, nor criticize her. He remarked, "My hands are damp," and she didn't quite make out what he meant. She read her poetry to him and he kept silent. He was sleepy when she explored his magnificent profile. "Shall we marry next Sunday?" she asked him and he said that Sunday was a day he wanted for himself. That was all.

"We should stop seeing each other," Dietrich said the next time they met. As usual, he left her a little gift, a gold brooch, but didn't say, "*Ich moechte mit dir sprechen*" Ivonne went to the Kleiner Weinkeller to drink a quiet beer in the rain and there was Hans-Jurgen, the computer geek, sitting at his usual table, his usual beer, Krombacher, almost black, in front of him. He didn't say "Hi" when she approached, but she sat opposite him. She said she didn't feel too well, but that was quite okay with her. He listened, drinking Krombacher, which was almost black. The street and its gray houses listened, and the evening was a poem about a woman who went to a pub, an old cozy place like no other in the world where a man should have waited for her. The evening didn't have anything good for the woman in the poem.

Ivonne took Hans-Jurgen to her tiny apartment, and he didn't say, "You are magnificent," the way the man in her poem did. He saw the jar full of rings, all of them much better than the one he had given her, and said, "You've worked hard." Then he was silent and she read "The Rhyme of the Ancient Mariner" which she had begun translating into German just for the pleasure of it.

Hans-Jurgen said, "Who, by the way, will you marry next Sunday?" and he didn't believe it when she answered she couldn't think of anybody.

Then it rained for two months and the sky was a pool of Krombacher beer, almost black. It was reassuring to have it there, Ivonne thought, above her poetry and translations, a big wet thing that gave her its cozy clouds. Her poetry didn't sell and her translations didn't make money, but that was all right. She went to Steigbuegel and if Hans-Jurgen was not there, she drank her Krombacher quite happily alone. Sometimes she recited her poetry to men she didn't know. They listened, and of course it was November and she missed Dietrich's beautiful, "*Ich moechte mit dir sprechen.*"

"You write well," the computer programmer told her once and she was happy. She was happy when after months of rain and Krombacher, Dietrich telephoned her. "*Ich moechte mit dir sprechen.* I'd like to have a word with you."

She had many things to tell him. One of her poems was published in a literary magazine. Her boss liked her translations and paid her. Hans-Jurgen had said again, "Let's get married next Sunday."

She had answered, "Okay," but this time she didn't go to the church Joseph Kirche because the rain was so thick and strong it broke her umbrella.

Dietrich's obedient skin gleamed in their old clean room above the Bavarian restaurant, and the night outside the windows was all happy winds. Dietrich had prepared a gift for her and said her poetry was okay. Then he said, "I want you to meet somebody."

Dietrich dialed a number on his mobile phone, and almost immediately the door of their clean room opened. A gangly youth entered, his thin body trembling, his cheeks red like the little lamp on the bedside table.

"Meet my son Volker," Dietrich said.

It was dark outside and she couldn't tell if the shadows she saw were silhouettes of houses or the evening was hauling new clouds in its wake. It was warm in the room and the TV was telling them it would be wet on the following day.

Dietrich patted the sickly boy's shoulder.

Ivonne thought of The Stirrup and of the poems she had written there. She had recited them to Dietrich and he had said "I hope Till will bring us the salad soon." Till was the waiter. He was slow or maybe the salad had not been ready.

The youth's hands trembled violently. His long blond hair trembled too. He produced a small packet out of his pocket. "This is a necklace," he said and scratched his meager neck.

He was sweating. His chin was covered with thin colorless hairs. "It's a necklace," the boy repeated.

His long trembling fingers reached for the buttons of

his shirt.

"What are you doing?" Ivonne asked.

"Come on," Dietrich said.

The boy took off his shirt. His puny chest glistened in the thin scarlet light of the bedside table.

"She is clean and she will teach you," Dietrich said glancing at Ivonne. "It won't hurt."

The boy recoiled and swallowed hard. Suddenly there were tears in his eyes.

You Play

"Don't take my clarinet, Vanko, please," Ivan said. "Do you remember when I played on it for your father? The old man's heart wasn't good, and his nerves were even worse. The nights gave him a nasty pain in the ribs. But I played him a song and he, well, you know what happened! He stretched himself out and limbered up. Look how battered the thing looks, Vanko." Ivan wore a frazzled quilted coat and clutched an old clarinet in his hand. It was evident the musical instrument had been through a lot of trouble; there were scratches and cuts all over its faded surface.

"You've been buying on tick for months now, Ivan," the man behind the counter said. "You haven't paid me back a single dime."

The men were in a poky room, a café, a pub and a convenience store all rolled into one. Vanko, its owner, sold the villagers rice, sugar and bread, which he drove from the town of Pernik in his pickup truck.

"I can't give your wife things on credit any more. When I see her coming, I lie to her that it's time to close the shop."

"Listen, I'll play free of charge at your son's wedding," the man in the quilted coat said, fingering the lusterless keys of the clarinet. "I'll play for free at the weddings of all your cousins, and I'll play for free at the funerals of all the old men in your clan. If you open a new shop or a new pub I'll play for nothing, gratis! You'll see. Send for me in the dead of night and I'll waste no time. I'll run over to your place like a rocket and I'll start performing. I can play at a wedding and I can play at a funeral. I can play for your new pub and for your old pub. Don't take my clarinet away. My son's learning to play now. The boy's got a sharp ear and strong lungs. He catches sounds from the streets and puts them in the instrument."

"You shouldn't drink so much, man. Why didn't you find a job in Italy? You should've made money instead of blabbering on about your kid," the tavern keeper said reaching towards the clarinet. "My son's young. He won't get married soon, and if my father dies, a dozen of bad eggs like you will turn up to play at his funeral just for the free beer, you know."

"Nobody can play like me, Vanko," the clarinetist said. "You know that."

It was cold in the room and the tile stove smoked. The smell of burnt logs mingled with the vapors of smoldering plastic bottles. Vanko wasn't a wastrel. He'd burn anything that he could burn to keep his shop warm. Rumors had it that he bought dead men's clothes and put them in the stove to save firewood in winter.

"When you threw a birthday party for your son, I played for him, free of charge and your wife cried," Ivan, the clarinetist, said. "And your father recovered after I played for him, although the doctor said the old man was just about to meet his maker. When the dentist pulled out your bad tooth, didn't you ask me to come and play for you? You were swollen like a bagpipe, but I played for you, and I killed the pain."

"You killed the pain because we got drunk together," Vanko cut him short. "And before you were done, you had sucked a bottle of my best brandy dry. Did you pay for it? No, you didn't give me a penny to bless myself with," the pub keeper muttered and reached out to collect the clarinet. "Look at it! It's fit for the junk-heap. Did you use that clarinet to dig in your garden with or what?" the pub keeper shook his head in disgust. "I wonder who I can sell it to. What else can I take from you, Ivan? Your TV rattles as if all its screws are loose. You can't even make out what you are seeing— a cow or a submarine."

"You can take…do you want me to give you my fridge?"

"That used to be my fridge, man. I threw it out and you went and collected it. I don't want the damn fridge."

"Then take the table from our kitchen. It's almost new. What do you say to that?" Ivan asked his voice strong with a new hope. "I'll put boards in the kitchen. The missus and I will make do with the boards. The kid's learning to play the clarinet now. He can play at weddings and he can play in your new pub. It would be a pity to take the thing away from him. He might become a big musician. He might play at the funerals of the big shots. His mother will cry her eyes blind if she sees that he has nothing to play on."

"I wouldn't drink like an eel if I was that interested in my son's dabbling with music. If I wanted my son to play at the funerals of the big shots, I wouldn't be bone idle like you, man. In the morning, your wife came to buy milk on tick. She already owes three months' salary to pay off her debts. What if her boss fired her? What if the dressmaking shop she works for went bust?"

"You can't sell my clarinet to anybody, Vanko. It's ancient. It belonged to my grandfather, you know. He played on it in Bucharest, Romania, and in Athens, Greece. Then my father played on it in Sofia for the miners and in Pernik, at Easter. I… I've played on it only here, in our village. Man, I tell you, who heard my tunes he forgot he was sick. Your own father…"

"No way. It's no use talking. What else can I take from you?" the café owner grumbled. "You are a loafer and a shirker. I'll nail that clarinet to the wall. Your grandfather and your father played on it. You drank it away. You know why some guys don't know chalk from cheese. It's because they drink. Their wives buy everything on credit, and before they are done they have spent three months of their pay!"

"Can I come here in the evenings?" Ivan asked, unbuttoning his quilted coat. "I'll take the clarinet down, and I'll play for a couple of minutes, no more."

"Do I look crazy to you? You'll scare away my clientele."

At that point the door of the pub opened and a boy, scrawny and weak, shorter than the counter in the pub, entered and joined the men.

"Like father like son," the pub keeper muttered.

"Manno, go tell your mother I can't sell her sugar on tick any more. Your father will leave the clarinet here and I'll give you bread for five more days. That's all."

The boy was silent. His eyes sank into the floor and remained there. Then he fumbled in his pockets, produced some small change, four cracked glass balls, a sling, and a clean handkerchief.

"Uncle Vanko," the boy began. "Take all these. Are they enough to buy Dad's clarinet back? This is the best sling in the village. And those are the hardest glass balls in the neighborhood. You can buy a bar of "Milka" chocolate on those nickels here. You only have to add forty-two cents and the bar of "Milka" will be yours."

"No way, Manno. Go home," the pub keeper said, scratching his head. Then he gave the boy a chocolate. "Take this, lad, and go home to your mother. There's a nip in the air. Run or you'll catch a very bad cold."

The boy fingered the chocolate, added it to the cracked glass balls, the sling and the small change, then took off his hat, hand-knitted with thick home-spun wool, added it to the rest of his possessions, and said, "Will you give me the clarinet now? Those things should be enough. And I'll come to sweep your pub first thing in the morning. Dad can play at your son's wedding free of charge. I mean when your son Dancho grows up. Dad can play at your father's funeral for free... I don't want Grandpa Boris to die, you know. I mean...I quite like him."

"Go home, Manno," the pub keeper said mildly.

"Let me play the clarinet for a couple of minutes," the

boy said. "Let me play then I'll bring our dog Rexi. I'll give him to you and you'll give me Dad's clarinet."

The pub keeper gave the boy the battered instrument which had played in Bucharest, Romania, and in Athens, Greece. It had played at all weddings and funerals in the village as well. The boy took it.

"Uncle Vanko," he said. "If your heart hurts, have no fear. It'll stop hurting after you hear me play. I promise!"

It was cold in the pub. The freezing wind howled outside and the air in the room smelled of burned plastic, cigarette smoke and smoldering beech firewood.

Quiet sounds trickled from the old clarinet: very soft ones, like the steps of a man who had recuperated from a long illness. Like the voice of a child who found a terrific penknife in the street. Like Athens, Greece, where the sun always shone, and like Bucharest, Romania, where it was winter now, but it was good all the same because in the houses the stoves burned and there was enough firewood; like sugar in your tea, like bean soup when you are hungry like a wolf. Like your mother's three salaries that she had not earned yet; like the two terrific glass balls and the best sling in the village. Like the wedding of Uncle Vanko's son who'd grow up after twelve years. Like wedding guests who drank a glass or two and were ready to dance till their heels burned. The lad's clarinet wouldn't stop until the oldest grandpa jumped and danced with the young girls.

Finally the boy stopped playing and the old clarinet once again looked battered and bruised. It seemed it had never seen Athens and Bucharest. It looked as though the hands of Ivan's father had never touched it, nor had the hands of Ivan who, to be honest, drank like a fish. Now the clarinet knew only about Ivan's debts.

The pub-keeper was not looking at the bottles on the counter. He didn't see the packets of sugar, and the big sacks of beans and rice. He didn't notice the stove in which the empty plastic bottles burned.

"Boy," the pub keeper said. "Take you clarinet and run back home. Tell your mother I'll bring you bread for one week. It will be on me! It's my treat! You play really great, boy!"

WINDS

"Will you go to Sylvia 's again?" her mother asked her more than a year ago.

"Yes," Veta said and went out.

That was how her fib-telling started and she'd kept it up ever since. There was no Sylvia . She named her loneliness Sylvia so her mother did not worry that Veta was alone all the time. Most often she remained in the library where the air smelled of beautiful paper dust, of poems which slept between the pages, of writers, forgotten long time ago between the thick dusty covers of the books. Veta knew them all. Her loneliness waited for her in the park, too; it was tucked down the long alley that started from Lolita café and led to the railway station: a very insignificant railway station where the fast trains from Sofia to Greece didn't stop, only the slow ones did, once a day. The trains rocked their wagons like dark clouds that moaned under the burden of human electricity. The alley was lined with poplar trees, their branches thick with ravens: black rivets that nailed the afternoon shut. She often walked along the narrow platform, sat on the bench on which dozens of guys had scrawled dirty words, and many "Ivan + Tanya = love," but Veta didn't read the dirty remarks and didn't calculate who plus who made love. Her loneliness was soft and quiet, there were ravens and sun in it and warm empty rails that reached the end of Bulgaria, and went on to the clouds in Greece. She called her loneliness Sylvia after that thin, black-eyed girl from second grade who she taught at school.

The girl still couldn't read. She managed to spell and utter only the short three-letter nouns but Veta loved the fairy tales the girl made up, tossing and pulling at those short, short words. Veta told the child, "Read this." Sylvia spelled out: "horse," "child," "moon" and the horse suddenly learned to fly. After a minute it hurtled off to the moon, where a little naughty child lived in a very peculiar house: its roof was built of sun's rays and its walls were white clouds. Veta's loneliness was a soft summer afternoon with rain in it, a small railway station, dark poplars, and ravens that knit in the clouds terrific nets of courage with their black wings.

"My mother is in Italy," the girl told her one day. "She takes care of an old woman there. My grandmother is here, in Bulgaria, and she looks after a toddler boy in Sofia. Listen, I hate the long words," Sylvia admitted. "The letters are too heavy for them and they can't run. I forget what they are up to while I spell them. That's why I can't read long words: I hate to wait for them while they linger in their places and can't move on. They have letters of stones —you can take my word for that."

"I wish I had grandchildren," Veta's mother often said. She had never married. She was a pediatrician in the small provincial hospital in Pernik and took care of the newborn babies. Many winters ago, a one-year old girl, Veta by name, was dying from viral pneumonia. The doctor didn't go home until the toddler gradually stopped running temperature and started sipping at its milk. Before the doctor adopted the child, she called her own loneliness Sofia after the capital of Bulgaria. After work, she went to the cinema or to theatre in Sofia, or simply mooned around the streets till after dinnertime.

"Perhaps we could think of somebody… a man you'd love to see or talk to," the pediatrician said to her daughter. "The management appointed a young neurologist in the hospital a couple of months ago. We could invite him to dinner."

Of course, they invited him to dinner but the man could stand neither the ravens nor the railway station. He adored long words that had many letters in them and couldn't run at all. His mouth transformed them into threatening diagnoses which could kill anybody. In the middle of the dinner Veta excused herself and left her mother and the young neurologist with their beefsteaks and sauté potatoes.

"Why did you do that?" her mother asked her in the morning. "It was not polite to run away on Doctor Tomov like that. You insulted him. Well… don't repeat my mistake, please. A woman should have a child. You simply… listen, find somebody for several weeks. Later you can go away. You and I will take care of the little one together."

"But…" Veta began. "No. I wouldn't like that."

"You call your loneliness Sylvia," the doctor said. "You've learned that from me. I'll ask Doctor Ivanov to dinner tomorrow. He's divorced."

"I won't be at home tomorrow in the evening," Veta said.

In the afternoons she remained in the teachers' room with Sylvia. The two of them read fairytales from Sylvia 's ABC book or solved problems about trains and sparrows.

"Miss Toneva," Sylvia said once. "You'd better have your own child because I learned to read long words. They are no longer full of stones. I even think some of them taste of chocolate. You can teach your child when you have one. What do you think?"

"It's not that easy…"

"Yesterday your Mom came to see me at school," the girl interrupted her. "Is it true you go to that small railway station every day? Why? The fast trains don't stop there and the canteen selling chocolate wafers is never open."

"I like the poplar trees," Veta said.

"Your mom asked me to find a guy who liked poplar trees and ravens for you," the child added.

"That would be silly," Veta said. "Now let's solve the problem about the two boats on page 67."

"Listen, I know such a guy. He's very tall. I'll show him to you. Your mom says she wants you to have friends. Look at me, I have many friends and I'm okay. Come on, I'll solve the problem about the two boats by myself. If it's too difficult, Grandma will help me. Look, is it true that you call the ravens, the station and the poplar trees after me? You can't call a raven Sylvia, and you can't call the rails Sylvia. Call them simply "station," "rails" and "ravens." Come with me."

Sylvia who looked small for her seven years and her teacher started off down the alley that went to Lolita café.

"Here he is," Sylvia said and pointed at the newsstand. A very tall man stood behind the heaps of bright pictures and titles of the newspapers. The girl rushed to him and said, "Here she is. She likes ravens like you."

The man fumbled in his pockets and gave the child a candy bar.

"No, I don't want it," the girl declared. "I love her. I didn't bring her here for your candies. I don't want her to stay alone with the rails. She'd better stay with you—never mind you are so tall."

Veta turned around and walked away down the alley.

"Hey!"

The man left his newspapers, caught up with Veta, reached for her arm and said, "That child's been telling me you like ravens. She's been repeating this for two months now."

"I have to hurry," Veta said.

"I love the railway station where you go every day. I've seen you there."

"I haven't seen you," Veta said.

"Sylvia offered to give me her box of crayons if I asked you out on a date. She said, 'You are very tall, but she'll like you all the same.' She also said you knew words that could fly."

Veta was about to leave when the newsagent added, "I want you to know that I need a box of crayons badly."

She turned around and looked at him, not knowing

what to say. The sky was thick with spring winds and the river flowed quietly not far away from the road.

"I wonder if I could buy you a cup of coffee this evening," the man went on. "If you are busy, I can wait."

His face waited. The winds and the spring waited, too.

Veta smiled. She didn't know why.

BAVARIAN STYLE

Any minute now, I expected that the man I was having dinner with would produce a letter typed on a sheet of yellow paper. I wasn't too happy about it, yet I tried to enjoy my Hare with Chestnuts Bavarian Style, sipping at my glass of fabulous Chardonnay d'Oc. The guy who had asked me out was very attractive. His Chardonnay was excellent, his dark suit was immaculate, his blue eyes were interested in me and his name was Udo Fischgrund. He was the senior manager of the company which dealt in a wide range of French, American and German cosmetics of worldwide repute.

I'd eaten half of my Hare Bavarian Style, yet the yellow letter I disliked with all my heart hadn't become a topic of our conversation so far. This made me feel uneasy and alert.

The reason why that letter gave me cold feet was, by all means, ludicrous. My mother was at the bottom of it all. She was a woman of character, that was all there was to it. If the old fair lady had something on her mind she was sure to get what she'd bargained for.

This sort of thing had happened to me quite a few times before, so I was well aware of the trap Mother had laid for me. She was good at making everybody around her suffer.

The turn the events would take as they followed the plan my mother had drafted always hit me hard. My admirer i.e. the man expected to propose to me, at a certain point at dinner would produce a letter scrawled or typed on a yellow sheet of paper. That particular tinge of the yellow color gave me bitter headaches. It exuded smells of the drawer in which my mother stored her cosmetics. I had the feeling the paper had absorbed the memories of all her wrinkles she had concealed under thick layers of rouge. To put it mildly, the yellow paper smelled of problems that Mother hoped cosmetics could resolve. So when my prospective husband asked, "What is this?" showing me the yellow letter, I sensed I'd lose the battle one more time.

The yellow document was the letter in which Mrs. Schwarzmuller, i.e. my mother, had thrown light upon the some remarkable facts. The epistle read:

"*Lieber Herr* (Dear Sir),

I doubt you have the vaguest idea about the woman you intend to share your future with. She is my only daughter, Sir, therefore I feel responsible for you. It was me who brought her up doing my best to share with her the human values of our civilization. I put in quotes the noun "civilization" because my daughter and the civilized world are totally incompatible entities. In short, she is a liar. If she says she loves you, *lieber Herr,* this can only mean one thing: you are a very rich man. She is after your money, believe me.

She is bound to squander all your assets
i.e. all your hard earned savings, Sir. She will
make you a beggar before you could say Jack
Robinson. In short, my daughter is a spend-
thrift. I'll reiterate that statement in clear con-
science in any court of law as the case may be.

I'd like to add she has lax morals. I've written those bitter words feeling utmost pain.
You can understand that, I am her mother. I
think I know what will happen to you; I have
already lived through similar circumstances
several times. Two other men before you, *lieber
Herr,* were credulous enough to welcome her
in their lives. Soon after that the poor guys,
God bless their souls, came to me complain-
ing of acute insomnia and lack of appetite.
She'd cuckolded them. Her ex-boyfriends suffered nervous breakdown. I, being a sensitive
woman, wept silently and lived in constant
dread of my high blood pressure. Therefore, I
ask you to put an end to your relationship
with my daughter. If you do not take my ad-
vice, you are sure to land in a psychiatric insti-
tution, and I, on my part, might as well meet
my Maker as a result of being hypertonic.
Alas, unfaithfulness is as indispensable to my
daughter as is water to a fish.

At the end of the first month of your
marriage, she will have fallen in love with another man. You are a sensitive guy—I can
somehow feel that. Therefore, *mein lieber Herr,*

run away on her if your future means something to you. Run for dear life while you are
still able to wrench yourself from her grip.

I wish you good luck with all my heart.
Please accept the assurances of my highest
consideration.

Extremely worried about you,
Mrs. Elfriede Schwarzmuller,
Victoria Schwarzmuller's mother."

At that point, the guy who had already bought an en-
gagement ring for me would stare at the yellow letter, rendered speechless.

More often than not my prospective husbands had asked
me to a romantic candlelit dinner, the usual eight candles
burning mystically, Vivaldi's "Spring" a magic in the air.
However, after the young man was halfway through my
mother's epistle, his face would grow thin and long.

As my first boyfriend read the yellow letter, he looked at
me, gasping in astonishment. His mother came to check
what the matter was and in no time there were tears in her
eyes. She pleaded with me to go away on my own accord.
The poor woman hailed a taxi for me and sent me packing
while my boyfriend sighed at the window looking pitiful as I
got into the taxi. My second boyfriend's father acted in a
somewhat innovative way. His son had received my mother's
letter, too. The text was identical, and it was only the date
that was different. The father, having adopted a businesslike
approach, informed me, "I make much more money than
Friedrich (the son). I've been looking for a woman like you."

Those words made the son start sobbing.

After that sad event, I made a pledge I'd have nothing to do with men who sobbed. So far, I had been as good as my word.

So far, Udo Fischgrund, the senior manager, had produced no yellow letter, and that fact instead of pacifying my troubled thoughts, made me choke on my Hare with Chestnuts Bavarian Style. It sounded highly improbable that Mother had let my present admirer slip unobserved from her eagle's eye.

The yellow smell of an old drawer seemed to hover in the air above my head. Udo smiled at me, the candles burned romantically, Vivaldi's Spring was again a magic in the air, and I suspected a trap.

"Your mother is a marvelous woman," said the man I hoped against hope to grow old with.

Two weeks ago, Mother dropped insightful hints that I'd die all alone, an author of best selling memoirs replete with red hot love affairs. I didn't like that. Finally Udo Fischgrund produced the yellow letter.

The moment of truth had come.

This time, Mother had written the following:

> "*Lieber Herr* (Dear Sir),
>
> You are a fortunate man: you have met my daughter, a magnificent woman. I brought her up and I am proud of her. She is my creation, a flawless creation, Sir.
>
> Victoria would never lie to anyone even if her life depended on that. If she says she loves

you it means that you are the love of her life and you will be the love of her life until she breathes her last. Loyalty is what describes best her character. Money is not of primary importance to her; however my statement should not be misunderstood: **she is not** a squanderer. On the contrary, Sir! Victoria is the thriftiest young lady I know.

She will successfully accompany you along the way to stable financial prosperity.

My daughter's love for you will be your safe haven, now and for good. It is the thought of the harmony between you two that stabilizes my dangerously fluctuating blood pressure.

I feel that she can make you very happy.

Please, accept the assurances of my highest consideration.

Mrs. Elfriede Schwarzmuller,

Victoria Schwarzmuller's mother."

P.S. *Lieber* Udo,

Thank you for sending me the high precision blood pressure/pulse measurement Eucerine device you and I talked about last month. I received it yesterday. Now I feel healthy, energetic and able to control my blood pressure under most untoward circumstances.

I simply adore the anti-cellulite apparatus you sent me for St. Valentine's Day! Could you believe the miraculous thing eliminated the abominable freckles on my hands that old age had given me? You have no idea how young I feel!

I was enchanted when yesterday you told me about the fibrinogen evaporator with which a lady can delete her wrinkles for good.

You are a serious scientist. I am proud of you!

Mit herzlichen Gruessen (All my best),
Elfriede

THE HAWTHORN BUSH

The first thing that struck me about Anna was her voice. Once I heard a woman sing one of those simple songs that the peasants in the mountain villages hum to keep wake in the long evenings. The song was about a young lassie who wanted her boyfriend to buy her a belt with a silver clasp. I knew that song and could say I'd never particularly liked it. But what a voice it was—it had all the silver of all the sliver clasps in the world in it, and it was bigger than the wind and it had the strength of a thousand belts in it. I'd never heard a voice like that. I was a keg maker and a barrel maker, but my heart wasn't in the hoops that held together the staves nor was it in the wine that the barrel held. I made taps that whistled when the wine passed through them and I loved it when I caught the sounds of the summer and of the wind in my gadgets. I made pen-whistles and tin-whistles for fun and I could listen for hours to their shrill piercing voices. A good voice in a silly song could make me freeze in my tracks. What I wanted was to capture the voice in my wine taps and make them sing.

My barrels were known everywhere in Bulgaria between the ridges of the Vitosha Mountain and the Rila Mountain, and that said a lot— the guys from the Vitosha mountain drank like eels on weekdays and like dragons on Sundays. Well, that was a pity because brandy ruined their voices. And their voices were deeper than the deepest lakes in the Rila Mountain, transparent like the water, and harder than the crags on the shore.

All those guys appreciated good brandy in a good keg and good wines in an old strong barrel of mine. I however had reached the point when I wanted an ordinary song more than a barrel. A song could turn the hot noon into a mountain peak for me, and a song could make the wind as tame as newborn puppy. I looked around. I wanted to be sure who the singer was. Alas, the only person I saw was the dark girl no taller than a keg for the weak hawthorn beer I made when I was drunk, or when I was in no mood to carve one of the magnificent barrels I was famous for. I couldn't believe what I heard. The small missy went on warbling about the belt with the silver clasps. Well, I was dumbfounded. Her voice was twice as big as her. I wondered where she produced it from—she seemed so meager and thin. The voice was like a hill with a hundred whirlwinds thrashing it, and at the top of that hill there was strong July sun that made the wind and the land pure gold. I listened and listened, and I said to myself, this can't be true. I was dreadfully sorry when the lass in the tune found her belt with a silver clasp and the song ended abruptly. The voice that was bigger than all the lakes in the Rila Mountain vanished into thin air and the wind died.

"Hey," I said, but she didn't turn to me. "Hey! Can you sing something else for me? I'll pay you."

She looked at me, her eyes the color of gunpowder about to explode any minute.

"Nobody calls me 'Hey', Mister. Let another 'Hey' sing for you," the girl said. "I'd remember that if I were you."

"I'm sorry, Madame," I said. There must have been a bite in my tone of voice for the young woman snapped, "I sing for no brazen-faced barrel maker even if he gave me all his filthy whistling casks."

"Oh!" I said. "Nobody has referred to me as a brazen-faced barrel maker."

"You are one," she said.

Then she was gone. I saw her narrow back, jumping and twitching and I caught a glimpse of her hair, curly and thick like a pile of thistles, bigger and heavier than the girl. She took her voice with her and suddenly I realized I'd lost something I could never retrace. I could put her song in my barrels and when the guys drank their plum brandy they'd have that mountain her voice had given the tune, and they'd have the big July sun and the bottomless dark lakes.

"Wait! Wait!" I called after her. "I'll give you my horse if you sing for me."

Everybody in these parts knew my horse Dorcho. He was red like the flames of one million candles and every hair shone a different shade of fire on his back. He galloped faster than an Opel car along the winding mountain roads and he had cost me four summers of barrel making eighteen hours of hammering and scooping and chiseling every single day. Those were happy summers, though. I made majestic vats and barrels that built a name for me no one could shake or steal. If a guy looked for "the barrel maker" it went without saying he meant me, Ivan the master of the singing casks. I'd hoped that runt of a girl would freeze in her tracks spell-bound on hearing the name of my whirlwind Dorcho.

"Ha!" she scoffed. "I wouldn't waste my spittle for a horse that's no better than a rag."

"What!"

"Rag," she said, the heap of her wild hair bobbing, vanishing like an owl that was chasing a rat amidst the beeches.

I went into one of my black huffs. I'd have no slandering mouths spitting and spewing lies about my thunderbolt Dorcho.

"Listen, hey!" I shouted at the top of my lungs which were very strong lungs of a barrel maker. "The mayor's daughter would be flattered I talked to her. Do you know what I'll do if I meet you again? I'll put you in front of my workshop to polish the shoes of my clients."

She must have heard me for after a minute or so she was again in front of me, looking me in the eye.

"And do you know what I'll do if I meet you again?" There was that smoldering gunpowder in her eyes that I happened to like.

"I'd very much like to know," I said waiting for her gunpowder to explode.

"I'll put you in front of the door of my room in the place of the doormat. First I'll wipe my shoes on you then

I'll talk to you."

"What!" The leaves of the beeches rang like church bells.

It was summer, the best time to make a keg from a dry walnut trunk for grapes bandy. The gapes and the walnut made good tunes in my whistles I put in the kegs. If the weather was windy the tune sounded sad and the guys who drank the brandy thought they were in store for a fight. But if the sun had stayed long enough with the wood and the brandy, the beech kegs sang. They remembered the roots of the trees, the branches, and the hill on which the beech forest used to grow. My whistles jumped with joy. That was what the sun was to my kegs. I had made kegs for many girls. I remembered a big keg I made for the mayor's daughter, and a small narrow one for the priest's daughter, and a low squat one for the daughter of the district police chief.

I often found a forgotten petticoat or a pair of lady's stockings under my bed. The girls were all pretty and each one of them deserved the barrel I made and the tune I put in it for her. No woman so far had said I was her doormat.

"A flea is bigger than you!" I shouted the summer and the leaves of the trees still dead church bells in my head.

She walked away and her back narrow as a cuckoo's nest sank into the bush. I felt like running after her.

Then I remembered I had found again a petticoat under my bed. The girl was the mayor's daughter and as usual I promised I'd make a barrel with a nice tune for her. Was it possible, I asked myself, to find the petticoat of one and the same girl every day and make barrels with good tunes for her? No, I'd be bored stiff! There should be different girls if I wanted new tunes and new barrels. I was sure of that.

The small girl, whose name I didn't know, stopped and shouted at me, "You goat."

"It's time you settled down," my mom said. "It's time I had grandchildren and not forgotten petticoats in our house." Then she heaved a sigh as deep as the sky before a storm and added sadly, "Your father was…well, I hate speaking about that," and she heaved another sigh.

"I will not have anybody call me a goat," I shouted back.

My mother was a gentle, quiet woman. She sang to me when I was a boy and she sang to dad when he was sick after he'd fought with other guys. I believed her songs made him strong again. He drank so much and ruined his voice that was powerful like a sledge hammer and sharp as a chisel. He was a brawler, and at times he screamed at mom but he was quiet when she sang to him, so I think that was why she sang to him, to keep him quiet. His eyes were as quiet as a room in which little children slept, and she sang, her soft voice making me guess dad had done something wrong. I was somehow sure she didn't like it at all, although she didn't say anything.

The girl walked along the path, all the light of the summer in her hair and all the blue of the sky in her long thick dress.

"Your dress is a rag," I told her. "Your shoes look even worse." She didn't say a word.

Mom never complained. Father was notorious far and wide in the valley of the Struma River and the old wives wondered how she put up with his numerous "female friends." I knew she often found petticoats and other things like lipstick or bottles of make up that didn't belong to her.

"Hey," I shouted after the minx of a girl with a storm and sun in her hair. "If you don't want to sing for me, maybe you will do something else with me. I've got a villa and I'll give you a golden necklace after that."

"Oh, will you?" She said, turning around. "Could you wait a minute, please?"

"Yes, I could. But why should I wait?"

"Because I need a sec to pick up a stone to hit your thick head with," she said and before I had time to wink she hurled the basket she was carrying at me. Then she walked away as calm as a hill all covered with snow, and as cold. I wondered how the big mountain was suddenly quiet under her feet and the grass she stepped on seemed to sparkle.

"Wait," I said, but she strode purposefully across the meadow, a mushroom that had suddenly learned to strut. "Hey, molehill, I'll break your basket." I called after her, brandishing the thing like a sword.

"Ha!" she sneered.

That was all I saw of that young lady that day and when I arrived at home I asked my mother after her.

"Well," my mother said. "I don't know which girl you mean. If she's the one I think she is, then you should be careful, son. She's got three brothers."

I passed many times by that stream where I'd met her but Molehill had vanished into thin air. I asked the shop

assistant in the clothes department after her, and I asked
the mayor's daughter. Molehill was on my mind all the time
I worked on a small keg from a trunk of a cherry tree I
had exchanged for three big bottles of my father's brandy.
I worked and I looked at the basket she had thrown at me.

And then one day I saw her herd of goats. The beasts
looked as meager as cats. They should have been very
hungry, the poor things, for the meadow looked as if a
razor had shaved the grass to the root in their wake. The
meadow was steep and there were crags jutting out of it,
and there were big thistles and thorns all over the place.
Above the meadow the mountain soared abruptly to the
sky, sharp, brown and huge. I noticed snakes and lizards
basking in the sun on the boulders. The clouds were flat
and hot, and it was a most ordinary and dull day—I could
make nothing but a pitiable barrel for the lowly brandy the
men in these parts made from half rotten tomatoes. We
drank such swill only when one of my friends got divorced
or when his wife ran away on him, or when his donkey
died in the middle of the road. That was a day for a barrel
to keep such hogwash in.

Then suddenly the big voice erupted amidst the goats.
This was no song. It had no words, it was just a huge endless voice that thrashed through the crags, beat the heat
and ran over the line where the hill ended and the horizon
began. I couldn't tell where her voice went or why sky was
suddenly in my hands. Her song glittered, big and deep and
long like a path to the place I had wanted to be all my life.
It felt like suddenly it was winter with deep snow, and at

the same time it was autumn and the trees were golden, and it was summer, too. There were church bells in her voice and there were hills and wheat grains. I stood transfixed. I listened and listened. The mountain became small. I had never seen so many winters and kids skating on icy rinks in a human voice. I never imagined a tune could hold a mountain, a summer and a herd of goats in it. My whole life was in that melody.

The song stopped abruptly.

"You again!" the angelic voice shouted. "Go away!"

The sky was flat, the winter was gone and the herd of goats attacked the steep meadow. That was the girl, this time her hair looked wilder if that was possible at all. I stared as she turned her back to me shooing her goats away.

"Hey!" I shouted. "Hey, marry me. Don't run away. Stay and marry me!"

She stopped.

"What?" she said. Her voice was small and her eyes were most ordinary brown eyes as she stood in front of me. Then I suddenly noticed her eyes were bigger than her, bigger than my whole life.

"I don't know your name, but it doesn't matter." I said. "Marry me!"

Her most ordinary brown eyes measured me and I knew they didn't believe me.

"I mean it!" I shouted.

"Ha," she said and pushed her goats up the thorns and thistles in the meadow. I followed her.

"Be tomorrow at 5 pm at Bitter Crossroads," she said

over her shoulder. "Don't forget to take an ax and a pick-axe with you."

"Bitter Crossroads?" I gasped. "You are out of your mind. There are only thorns, thistles and hawthorns there."

"I mean it," she said.

"What! What do you mean?" I asked her but she pushed her goats, disciplining them with her thin stick. She paid no attention to me.

Bitter Crossroads was a lousy spring that ran dry in summer and spewed muddy water and sleet in the autumn that tasted bitter in your mouth if you were crazy enough to taste it. In winter, the thing turned into a thick shield of ice that covered the whole hill. The place was thickly over-grown with hawthorn shrubs and sloe-thorns, and the path that squirmed its way to the spring seemed as narrow as the eye of a needle to me. It was hot, and the ax and the pickaxe I carried weighed a ton each. I had tied my horse Dorcho a mile away from the wilderness and all the way to Bitter Crossroads nettles, thorns and prickles clawed at me and tore at my shirt. It was half past four, I'd come too early, but I was all ears. Perhaps Molehill was nearby? I could hear her steps if I was lucky.

Well, if the guys who bought my kegs saw me here at the back of beyond, they'd make fun of me until the day I breathed my last. And they'd be perfectly right. I was wait-ing for a mushroom, I didn't know her name and I'd told her I wanted to marry her. As a matter of fact, I'd thrown hints a number of times it was about time I settled down in the presence of the mayor's daughter and wife.

I'd been walking two hours to get to Bitter Crossroads in the scorching heat, dragging a pickaxe and an ax, damn it. Didn't I have a screw loose? It was ten past five and no Molehill was in sight. I fidgeted, sweated and cursed under my breath. What a fool I was, what an idiot! I stared at the endless thorny shrubs, at the hole that used to spew brown mud, and I chewed my lip. It was twenty minutes to six. The ax and the pickaxe lay useless at my feet.

"Hey, barrel maker!"

Wasn't I startled! I looked around and I saw nothing, no Molehill, no Mushroom, nothing.

"Where are you?"

Then I saw her. She was amidst the thickest shrubs, her old long, long dress showing nothing of her legs.

"I was here all the time, barrel maker."

"No!" I said. "I was listening and I was watching."

"Didn't I hear somebody mutter he was a damned fool and an idiot?" she said her most ordinary brown eyes on my face. Suddenly they were the most extraordinary eyes I'd ever seen.

Then I was angry.

"You sneaked up on me like a snake," I said seething.

"You said you wanted to marry me," she said.

"Yes," I admitted. "So what?"

She said nothing. She ran into the wood, grabbed a big hawthorn shrub, her arms pushing through the branches, her old long dress sticking to the leaves, her wild hair mixing with the barbs and prickles of the damned thing.

"If you want to marry me," she said, "You have to

wrench me from that bush first."

"Oh, come on," I said. "I won't have bullshit like this."

"It's your choice," she said, plunging her fingers deeper into the thick sharp leaves amidst the prickles.

I took a step to the hawthorn tree and a couple of nettles stung my bare legs. I retreated rapidly towards the dead spring.

"You are not much of a man, barrel maker," the girl scoffed amidst the hawthorn branches.

I advanced to the shrub taking no heed of the nettles, but the spiky twigs, sprigs and their barbs dug into my cheeks.

"I told you to bring an ax and a pickaxe," she said.

I grabbed her long dress and pulled. The garment came apart at the seams and a piece of the rough cloth remained in my fists, but Molehill clung to the hawthorn bush like a horseshoe to Dorcho's hoof. It was hot, and the prickles of the small tree stuck into my hands. I could see her little face. It appeared as calm as 20-year- old brandy sleeping in my best barrel. She waited unperturbed, reserved and remote as if I wasn't sweating to get to her.

"You are not even beautiful" I shouted.

Her face remained aloof and I knew the brandy in her eyes wasn't meant for me. Well, Molehill, you don't know me, I thought to myself. I reached out, caught hold of her arm and pulled hard. The minute I thought I'd got the better of her she bit me. Weren't her teeth sharp as chisels! And sharper! I let go of her arm.

"Use the ax and the pickaxe," she said her voice quite dry and matter-of- fact.

I lifted the pickaxe and tried to cut off some damned

branches, but I cut my leg instead. Then a thought crossed my mind: if I felled the tree, couldn't I drag Molehill, leaves, spines and all? I hit the branches, beat at the trunk, sweated and thrashed about, then finally saw it would be easier if I uprooted the damned shrub. I started digging a big ditch around the thing while Molehill clung to the thorny branches, her hair entangled with the twigs. I dug the hole, and started chopping and clobbering the trunk. It was a thin bush, nothing strong or sturdy, so I cut it off in no time.

"It would've been easier if you'd simply asked me to climb down," she said.

I didn't answer. I didn't care that the spines had scratched and scraped my nose. There were splinters in my toes and my fingers tingled, but I could live with that. I clutched at the hawthorn bush and at Molehill who clung to it, then I shouldered the bundle of thorny branches, torn dress and wild hair.

"Now you can ask me to walk you home," she said and smiled. I thought it was the first time she smiled for me. Her smile was big like the sky and the wind in it.

"You and the bush are not heavy at all," I said. "I can carry you both to the top of the mountain."

Her smile was gone and there was no more sky above my head.

"Sing to me, please. Sing to me."

There was the big smile on her face again half hidden behind her endless hair.

She sang. The mountain under my feet froze in its

tracks. The wind listened. It was a very simple song, the one about the girl and her old belt. It was a great song. Her voice was thousand times richer than my all singing barrels. My whole workshop was dust compared to the old belt in Molehill's song.

Then suddenly she stopped singing and I didn't know where I was. I saw her smile waiting for me. The old belt in her song loved me. The mountain top was my brother and waited for me, too.

"I can't live without you," I whispered. "I simply can't. I wouldn't for all the barrels I made."

"I know," she said.

She tried to kiss me, but her enormous hair was all over the place, entangled with the branches of the hawthorn bush I'd just uprooted. I kissed her. There were some spikes that were in the way, but I could live with them. In fact, I couldn't. I couldn't kiss her big and long the way I wanted.

"Here he is! Here! This way!" I heard men's voices shouting. "What is he doing to her!"

Her two brothers, not very tall, but stout and sturdy, rushed to me, very dangerous with their axes and cudgels, their eyes burning like branding irons.

"We'll kill you like a pig!" the bigger one shouted. "Anni, did he do anything to you?"

"I'll cut his ears, I'll cook them and I'll make him eat them!" the smaller one yelled very bloodthirstily, brandishing his ax. "Come here, Anni, come!" he urged her.

"Quick," the bigger brother chimed in. "Let us save

you fist. We'll kill him later."

Molehill suddenly ran away from me and I thought, "It's over. She's gone." Everything became gray. The world was a dark place and I didn't care if they beat me black and blue or they cooked my ears and made me eat them. Then Molehill suddenly grasped another hawthorn bush, a smaller one this time. She clung to the stem, clasping it, her fingers caught hold of the spiny branches, her dress stuck to the thick leaves, her hair was all over the place bushier than the hawthorn bush.

"Come here or I'll break your head!" her smaller brother thundered.

"Break it if you can," she said calmly.

"Let's first kill him, and then save her," the other brother offered as the two of them stared at me. It was suddenly very hot. The sky reeled, the mountain shook and the only thing I saw was the bigger brother's cudgel and the smaller one's ax.

"I'll stay with him!" Molehill said. Her brothers froze in their tracks. I froze too, but then the air was suddenly so wonderful and the sky was my friend. The wind was my brother, and the mountain peaks loved me. The magnificent summer waited in my hands.

"What!" the bigger brother screamed.

"What!" the more bloodthirsty one bawled.

"You have to extract me from the tree if you want to take me home," Molehill told them. "Or you can tear the bush by the roots."

"You are off your rocker," the more thickset brother

muttered trying to seize her hand. "Ouch!"

"Ouch!" the second brother screamed, trying to pluck out the thorn from his thumb.

"Tell them you love me," Molehill turned to me. "Tell them you can't make your barrels without me."

"Shut up!" the brothers roared in unison.

"He's after the mayor's daughter!" screamed the one.

"And you are dirt under his shoes!" thundered the other.

"I love her!" I thundered back. "I don't want to live without her. I don't want to breathe without her…I can't walk without…"

I'd forgotten the younger brother's cudgel. It hit my head as the ax of the bigger one bit my shoulder. I'd forgotten everything, but then their fists were at work.

"If you hit him one more time," Molehill was shouting. "I'll tie both of you while you're sleeping, I'll drag you to the river and I'll drown you in the pool!"

All of a sudden her brothers stopped beating me.

"She'll sure do that," the elder one ventured. "You know her."

"Yea," the other one said. "I know her."

"Hey, idiot," the younger brother barked at me. "Get out of here before I kill you."

I could have hit him in the face. I knew that after my blow his face would be a heap of broken bones, smashed nose and tattered skin. I didn't clobber him; after all he was Molehill's brother. The air was still wonderful and the mountain peaks were still my brothers. Molehill was there smiling, her black eyes full of summer, her smile a light, happy breeze in my heart.

"I love you, Molehill!" I cried out.

Her brothers stood in her tracks, staring at me the cudgels and axes idle in their hands.

"I love the tunes you put in your barrels, Ivan," she said.

It was the first time she'd pronounced my name, and I froze in my tracks too. "I love these tunes. They are so beautiful."

The mountain was a song, the hawthorn shrub was a song and Molehill's hand felt magnificent on my arm. And she was beautiful, so beautiful I could hardly say another word.

Narrow Street

Most of the time, I felt peaceful. I rarely talked to anybody. I had always lived in unstable silence, winters hurling snow and rain at my windows, passing unnoticed and unnecessary. Probably, my next-door neighbor thought I was a queer fish, I could tell that by the way she stared at me when she met me at the grocery store. I'd been living in this neighborhood for five months. I chose that room with a window to the North tucked away down a narrow street. All the houses here were small and you could scarcely see them in the fog. There was fog everywhere: on the roofs, in the trees, in my hair and coat. The sun gave birth to fog instead of mornings.

I thought I was a bad company so I kept myself to myself, going for interminable strolls in the wasteland surrounding the only bridge in town. I tried to remember the outlines of the low squat buildings as they slowly dissolved into the afternoons like memories of a snowstorm. Sometimes guys whistled at me. The town was not big, people knew each other and I was a complete stranger in it, like a new poster advertising a concert in the main street.

I guessed the townsfolk unanimously mistrusted me when they got to know I what I did for a living. Even before the end of the first month of my sojourn in the narrow street, I gained a steady notoriety as an unbearable teacher in mathematics. I wanted the students to prove theorems and solve problems. I didn't speak much to them. Even on the first day at school, I caught two guys cribbing from finely folded sheets of paper they had tucked up their sleeves. The bad thing about me was that I saw and heard most of what happened in the classroom. I could almost always tell when a guy was trying to cheat. When I was a little girl, even grandma could not trick me into believing that dad had gone on a long business trip to Greece to make money for us. I knew he had divorced mother. A year after that I knew mother would not come back home to see me as she had promised after uncle Ivan took her to hospital for some blood tests. I tried to keep a stiff upper lip but all I managed to do was to bite my lower one that had long ago become very thin and colorless.

The only place I talked was the classroom when I examined my students. I hated to see guys copying from their neighbors. I took the neatly folded sheets of paper with the formulae from their fists and kept them on my desk. I supposed it was mortifying to be stared at by your math teacher but I couldn't think up anything else.

My classes hated me. I saw it in their eyes and everything I said seemed short, stiff and formal. I felt awkward every time I met a student I knew as he sauntered by, the fog making me freeze in my tracks in front of the bridge between the wilderness and me.

One Wednesday, I asked one of the students to prove the theorem about raising the diagonals of a rhombus to the second power. I watched him closely as he tore the sheet from his textbook and started for the blackboard. He began to copy the theorem from the sheet not even trying to conceal what he was doing. He printed the words slowly, unfalteringly, taking peeks at me behind his shoulder. I gave him a poor mark.

"*Assiez vous!* Sit down," I said.

He remained in front of the blackboard, calm, tall, writing the formulae, his fingers sifting out the chalk powder. He copied the theorem to the end and bowed to the class. The students applauded vigorously, some laughing, others smirking. I wished the fog was with me now, but it was a mile away and I thought I'd never again make it to the wilderness. I didn't know what to do with my eyes and my hands, I panicked I'd start to cry. It turned out I had dropped the piece of chalk some time ago and I saw it at my feet on the floor. It was very hot in the room. Words failed me, I stood there, mute like the fog, egg on my face. I was scared my voice would sound gravelly and they all would dissolve into laughter. They watched on, perfectly silent. I staggered to the blackboard and gripped another piece of chalk, then started dictating slowly, the words dead on my lips, "The diagonals of a rhombus..."

The students listened. I hoped they had not noticed how dry my voice was or perhaps they were accustomed to it that way. Suddenly, the boy I had given a poor mark jumped from his desk and sent his bag crashing to the floor.

"Excuse me," he said, strutted to my desk, took my piece of chalk and left without closing the door.

All the rest were silent, watching me. I checked the boy's name in the register. He was called Michel.

That day I had four more lessons that weighed a ton each. I felt squashed; in fact every day I left school exhausted as if I had dragged crags and stones from the slate-quarry in the hill to my living room. I had a headache. The schoolyard, the shops and birches were brown silhouettes, and the town was whispers and whirring of motors through which my headache and I walked. I reached my narrow street where the houses were neat and immobile mussel shells.

The small square in front of the cottage where I lived was my medicine. It ended abruptly at the foot of a hill overgrown with shrubs and thorns that mixed with the autumn and its starless sky. I wanted a cup of tea, and I wanted my warm room where I forgot the classroom, the town and the theorems. Every evening I lit all the lamps and celebrated the absence of fog and blackboards around me. I had counted the steps that separated my room from the schoolyard. It was fun counting the yards that I had to go before my cup of strong tea.

Suddenly, somebody whistled at me. I jumped. I rarely met people in my narrow street, silence felt like the ocean floor here. The face, which popped up in the fog before me, gave me the creeps. It was the student I had given a poor mark, Michel.

I walked slowly on, aware of strange noises. I soon realized there were two more guys I didn't know with Michel. I crept on, forbidding myself to turn back, feeling their words and breaths on my neck. I was not scared, not in the least. I could hear their light footfalls behind my back. When I was a little girl my grandmother used to leave me at home by myself when she gave lessons in maths to students at their homes. I was accustomed to silence and I knew it was my friend. The three guys stalked me, silent like the brown clouds. I had lived alone and I was not afraid of footsteps in the dark. I reached the front door of the house where I lived, turned around and looked at them. They stared back.

I entered the house and closed the door. It was quiet and warm inside.

On the following day, Michel walked out of the classroom in the middle of my lesson. He was humming a familiar tune for quite a time. When I asked him to stop he winked at the class, then left.

In the afternoon, Michel and the other two guys trailed after me while I walked along the street paved with anxiety and fog. I wished I could dash off, yet I wasn't scared. It was dark and I could hear their shoes hit the pavement. One of the three guys, the tallest among them, with the swarthy face, caught up with me, halted and looked me in the eye.

"I'd like to tell you something," he said. His face, long and thin, almost touched mine. He cleared his throat.

"I have never met a girl like you. You have a good figure. *Vous êtes jolie..*" His dark eyes measured me slowly. "You have a beautiful voice. Your eyes are beautiful."

A thick stream of derision oozed from his words. Michel and the other guy were only a step away from us, watching me, snickering. The swarthy one was snickering too. Suddenly, he let out a loud guffaw. I did not mind that. I could endure anything. I looked at him then turned and went on down the street. The mussel shell houses waddled in the dusk making it jagged and menacing. I reached the small square, the shrubs and the wilderness. This time my well-lit room and my cup of strong tea were no good.

In the morning I had a headache that became excruciating during the five lessons with my classes. I dictated the problems and repeated the theorems, trying to ignore the waves of uneasiness as best as I could. Finally the lessons were over and I walked slowly out of the school yard.

The three guys were waiting for me at the beginning of my narrow street. They roared with laughter the minute they saw me. I hurried past them, trying to remain composed.

"I'd like to tell you something," one of the guys shouted. I didn't stop. I noticed his eyes were the color of the fog, watery, cold. "*Vous êtes jolie.* I have never met a girl like you before. You have a good figure. You have a beautiful voice…" Suddenly he was short of breath and looked at Michel and the swarthy guy for support. I didn't wait for the remaining part of the explanation.

"Will Michel be the next one?" I asked.

My question was greeted with jeers. I ignored them. My eyes were beautiful, I knew that. I left the guys where they were and walked down the narrow street feeling their eyes on my back.

I went home and tried to get some sleep. The fog and the town were blue behind the windowpanes. In the morning before I went to work, I found the three guys in the square with the bridge to the wilderness. The swarthy guy and Michel came striding along to meet me.

"I'd like to tell you something," Michel said. He looked away, blushing.

"I won't listen to you," I told him.

"I have never met a girl like you," he started. "You have a good figure. Your voice is beautiful. Your eyes are beautiful, too…" Then he didn't know what to say. He looked at the bridge for help, hoping I'd go away. I waited.

"Her hair is beautiful, too," the swarthy one gave him a clue, whispering. His words, sharp and edgy, cut his face into two halves.

"Tomorrow I'll wait for you at 7 pm in front of my house," I said.

Michel coughed, the swarthy guy stared, surprised.

"She's up to something," the swarthy one muttered.

Perhaps my neighbor had seen me and was wondering what I was discussing with these young men. I took a step forward. I had to go to work.

"What did you say?" Michel asked.

I did not answer.

"Hey, what did you say?" the swarthy guy cried out, his voice indignant. "You'll wait for me, is that it?"

I didn't answer him. I knew I had one thousand steps more before I reached the classroom.

"What did you say?" The swarthy guy caught up with me.

"Tomorrow at 7 pm," I said so quietly he had to bend if he wanted to hear my words.

That day I examined many students, I spoke slowly, avoiding their eyes. I didn't look at Michel.

At 7 pm sharp I was in front of the house where I lived. The swarthy guy had already arrived. The other two boys were a couple of yards away from him, hiding behind a clump of pine trees. This time they were not laughing. They watched me. I watched them, too, and I was not scared.

The swarthy guy waited, his hands thrust into his pockets. I came up to him, nodded, studying his face. It was very smooth and dark. He kept silent as I watched him run his fingers through his hair. It was black and thick.

"*Bon jour*," he said at last.

The other two guys had pushed aside the branches of the pine trees. They waited, ready to start sniggering. Suddenly I hated them.

"Stop fidgeting," I told the swarthy guy.

He stared, confused. I caught him by the shoulders, stood on tiptoe and kissed him.

I hated Michel and the other guy. I hated the man I had just kissed and I couldn't stand the fog. I had already taken my revenge on them. No sound of steps chased me, no one guffawed. The fog and the pavement were peaceful. The mussel shell houses smiled at me with their cloudy roofs.

I entered the classroom. It was very peaceful in it, too. The students looked at me in a very peculiar way, their eyes quiet like my evening cup of tea. As always, I started the lesson with a new theorem leaving a storm of chalk dust in my wake. Michel smiled and that made me feel awkward. I felt ashamed of myself and stopped turning back to look at them.

After the lessons were over, the swarthy guy waited for me near the bridge, which led to the fog. His two friends were not with him.

MISS DANIELLA

She had a rule: everything had to be clear and simple. It meant she paid you well and used the service you offered her. Wiser people had thought of that a long time ago. Daniella never deceived her workers; she gave them every penny of their wages on the 17th of the month, and they, after plodding away at the weeds in the fields, grumbled without looking at her, "Thank you, Ma'am."

They were stubborn and baked in the sun like bricks. They wouldn't say "Thank you" to the doctor who extracted the bullet from a wound in their bellies, but they thanked Daniella because her bundles of banknotes were stronger than their heads and thicker than the dirt under their nails.

Daniella's land was boundless; she had inherited it from her grandfather: rich fertile soil, overgrown with grass that remained green throughout the summer on the northern slope of Shar Mountain. There, the last snowdrifts thawed at the end of July. At all other places, snakes hissed and lizards mated. Miss Daniella, as hard as the marble roof-tiles above her house, had made up her mind to get very rich here, in the wilderness. She sowed her fields with wheat, maize, barley, and fruit.

Her seven workers, working their fingers to the bone in the valley among four hills, lived in the building that used

to be her grandfather's summer manor. He used to ac-
commodate his young mistresses in it, but now the place
exuded a pungent smell of dead creatures, forgotten in the
rooms. The farmhands tilled the land in the spring, summer, and autumn. Daniella knew what held them here: the
bundles she brought them on the 17th of each month. She
was an odd woman and made it a point of making her
men shave the bristles on their chins and cheeks when she
paid them. She looked satisfied on hearing their obedient,
"Thank you so much, Ma'am."

Sometimes in the evening, she saw them in the thirsty
summer, sitting by twos or threes on the ground under the
linden tree, bottles of cheap brandy in their hands. Actually, you couldn't really call it brandy. It was a sour, scorching concoction made of turnips that clouded your head
like a brick. Daniella sold the true plum brandy abroad, in
Greece or in Serbia. At her pub, The Maupassant, she sold
the cheapest brandy an honest man could dream of. The
same workers, their bruises still fresh, brewed the brandy
from Miss Daniella's plums and pears, and paid for it at
The Maupassant. They drank and talked, but she didn't
listen to them; she knew their words were mostly strings of
obscenities. The politest expression for a woman they used
was "slut." They described in detail what this or that hussy
did for them and how much it cost them.

There was a tart in these parts named Boryana. The guys
swore at her less harshly when she came in the evening to
The Maupassant. Boryana usually came after the men fed
the pigs. She sat directly on the grass, the blades dirty and

116

squashed under her overalls, and she, too, drank from her hip flask. If it was Tuesday, she chose a guy from their group of unshaven farmhands, all of them smelling of dust, sweat, and horses, and took him behind The Maupassant.

On Tuesdays, Boryana, the girl the workers swore at softly, as if they were telling her "Good evening," took one of them to the backyard where crates of beer bottles and brandy were stored. On Tuesdays, she didn't charge the guy. Sometimes it happened that Boryana chose the same worker on two consecutive Tuesdays, but the other boys didn't grumble. They waited for their turn, drinking. Boryana carried an ax tied to her waist, and she had a gun, too. Once, she cut a piece of a guy's ear because the smart aleck had tried to run away before he paid her. Without the slightest hesitation, she roasted the piece of the ear, saying she did this as an example for all of the other farmhands.

Because of that, Daniella came to realize that Boryana was worth a kingdom and hired her to work at The Maupassant selling brandy, the beer, the packs of cigarettes, and canned goods, mostly canned sprat. That was the cheapest fish in these parts, and the farmhands loved it. They all were as tight-fisted as tongs. They squandered money on brandy, but it never crossed their minds to buy sprat, for they gorged themselves on Daniella's fruits. Of course, no one paid her for those. They ate like elephants and perhaps had already gobbled down a twelve-wagon train of her fruits but she couldn't order them to stop bolting apples and peaches, nor could she keep an eye on them all the time. The guys saved up every cent they laid their hands on. They caught grass-snakes that blissfully basked in the sun, skinned them, and roasted them. Boryana cooked grass-snake meatballs and rice at The Maupassant, and in the evenings she drank and sang with the boys.

"Why don't you charge them on Tuesdays?" Miss Daniella asked Boryana once.

"What?" Boryana said.

"Why don't you take money from them on Tuesdays?" Daniella explained.

"Then I don't work. It's my pleasure, "Boryana said. "A woman should have fun from time to time."

"What if one day they killed you?" Miss Daniella asked.

"Who will they go to the backyard with then? With the grass snakes, perhaps?" Boryana answered. "Who else will charge them so cheap? We live at the back of beyond here, there's no other woman a guy could break his fast with. The two old wives in the neighboring village are pushing the daisies. Only you and I stay here, Daniella. But you are rich."

So Boryana was a blessing in disguise for everybody in the manor. How come she dragged herself to these desolate hills? No one could tell for sure. Perhaps she had bumped off a guy in Pernik and hid among the three mountains, or she had stolen someone's money and frittered away every penny on poker? Whatever the truth, the farmhands were extremely pleased with her. She had established firm working hours: 11-12 am, and well after midnight, 2-3 am at latest. She charged them 1 lev, and sometimes she allowed them to come to her backyard on credit, until 17th, when Daniella paid them. Boryana didn't even write down how much money they owed her. She cut a notch with her knife on the bar of The Maupassant and knew exactly each guy's debt. When Tuesday came she chose Kalinko and took him to the crates and the empty brandy bottles where her home was.

She had tamed the men with her ax, which she never removed from her skirt. Every once in a while, when she was still sleeping at 11 am, they brewed coffee and made sandwiches for her, especially if a guy's shoe pinched him badly and he was itching to bring breakfast to her. Boryana kept her gun under her pillow, but when Miss Daniella asked the farmhands what they thought about Boryana, the guys said Boryana was worth a heap of gold or even more heaps, because if she went away from The Maupassant, they would slit and slash each other's throats. Everything was all right with her and it was fabulous on Tuesday nights.

Daniella lived in her father's house, an imposing two-story dwelling which turned its blind walls on the northern slope where the snow didn't melt well into July. All the windows, except the two narrow ones, had been boarded up. Their dusty windowpanes offered a view to the lake where Miss Daniella went to swim. She had forbidden her farmhands to bathe in the water because she bred trout in it. Daniella made a lot of money on the trout and bought many books, all turning gray with the thick peaceful dust on them, she had a TV, a VCR, and a piano that looked gray, and the dust on them was ankle-deep. In the evening she, dog-tired after patrolling up and down the fields, sour with constantly digging at her farmhands, at 9 pm had a swim and went to sleep.

"You can move into one of the rooms in the manor," Daniella said once to Boryana. "You'll give me ten levs per month, which is a ridiculously low rent."

"Are you crazy or what!" Boryana had almost shouted at her. "Ten levs! Do you know how long I have to lie on my back to make Ten levs! I'll never give you that much."

"Okay, five levs per month," Daniella said. "You can't imagine how unbearable it is to be alone in an empty house. The stars snarl at me like that dog that died on account of the putrid fish I gave him. The moon shines and scares the trout all through the night. You have no idea how horrible that is."

"You are right. I have no idea," Boryana said. "I've never been alone. Look here, you stay alone in that big house of yours while seven men whine like the dog you poisoned with the rotten fish. It's a crime. I hate to think about the way they suffer. They're my friends, all of them, even Velin is. I've cut the price. Now I charge them half a lev. They are short of money, but they all want to get married after the autumn is over."

"Okay then," Daniella said. "Move into the manor. You won't have to pay any rent. We'll watch movies on the VCR together."

"But I work until 2 am. Your VCR will come to bits while you wait for me," Boryana pointed out. "You pay me my salary and I sell your brandy, your beer, and cigarettes, that's true. You have to know that if you give me the sack, I'll survive. I'll have roasted grass snakes for lunch, and the boys will sit on the ground and not on the mattress you gave me. You know the mattress: you told me your grandpa met his maker, lying sick on it. I ask you fair and square: how can you live on a TV and on books? You can't live on books. Why don't you start charging the men…let's say 1 lev and 20 cents? You are more learned than me and you deserve more. What's fair is fair. They are as stingy as graves. They won't give you more than 1 lev and 20. You look pretty enough to me, though. You could charge them 1 lev and a half. I guess nobody's going to shell out 2 levs for you."

"Will you move into the manor?" Daniella whispered. "It is not the men I am interested in, Boryana, it's you."

"It's okay with me if you love women, Daniella, but I won't move in with you. There are seven farmhands I have to think of."

"I'd just like to have someone to talk in the evenings," Daniella said. "That moon makes me crazy. It's glued to the sky like a roof-tile. Some day it will drop onto my head."

"I don't see anything wrong with the moon," Boryana said. "We've been shooting the breeze…I could have made 5 levs so far. Can't you hear the boys swearing? Try to understand them. You haven't started swearing in this heat. It's a wonder."

"I have, but I don't do it in front of everybody. All right, then, can you recommend one of the farmhands to me?"

"What exactly do you want me to do?"

"Recommend a guy to me who gives you half a lev."

"You want me to explain what we do?" Boryana did not understand. "I do everything I feel like doing and I feel like doing a dozen of things at a time. Daniella, if you stopped riding that scatter-brained Balzac horse of yours through the fields, you, too, would feel like doing things. Start selling brandy like me. It could help."

"You think I don't want to?" Miss Daniella muttered.

"Let me tell you one thing: your brandy's lousy, Daniella. Just between you and me, it's a shame you make me sell that brandy. You should pay the guys if they agree to drink it."

"To recommend a farmhand to me means to tell me who among them takes baths most often."

"All of them do. They swim with your trout. They catch trout and I grill the fish for them. Daniella, I, too, want to make a lot of money. I'll work one more month and I'll say goodbye to this place, full stop!"

"What do you want to make money for? Tell me. Maybe I can give you higher pay."

"I want to get married. Then I wouldn't have to charge the guy 1 lev. I'll do it for free, the way the water flows in the stream… He'll be my husband. Do you understand? And I'll do that not only on Tuesday."

"I don't understand," Miss Daniella said.

"The boys are my friends. I like to make them happy. That's why I love Tuesdays. Look, I've chosen one guy: Kalinko. You can say he's too scraggy, but he's the strongest one. Before he goes to sleep, he tells me, "You are pretty, Boryana. I want to look at you a minute more."

"Who's Kalinko?" Daniella asked.

"The guy with the scar between his eyebrows. He's as meek as a dirt road. He's the only one I trust and I untie the ax from my ass when I'm with him. The others seem to be meek, too, but you remember that guy whose ear I cut. You never know, it might be necessary to cut another ear one of these days."

On August 17th, 1 pm sharp, Daniella came to *The Maupassant* with the money. The men were listening to Turkish belly-dancing music and, despite the heat, some stirred restlessly. Those languorous tunes were no old wrinkled women one could turn a deaf ear to. The Turkish belly-dancing tunes were splitting the air when Miss Daniella came riding Balzac, her chicken-brained horse. She wore a white flowing dress, white sandals, white broad-brimmed hat, and white gloves. Balzac's hide and mane were sparkling white, too.

"Have you made up your mind? Will you move into the manor or not?" said Miss Daniella looking at no one in particular.

"Yes, I have made up my mind," Boryana answered. "I won't come to the manor. The boys need me here."

Daniella took a fat bundle out of her bag and she paid Boryana first.

"Have you weighed up the pros and cons?" Daniella insisted.

"Yes, I thought things over and now I tell you: I'll remain with the mattress you grandpa died on. Every night the guys and I bring it back to life. One forgets one's been digging the cornfields for hours after his back settles down on that mattress."

"Okay," Daniella said and started paying her farm-hands. Her nails were varnished a dazzling shade of white, and she didn't smell of Balzac the chicken-brained horse, she didn't smell of books or of dust, nor did she smell of the winds and fields she had crisscrossed on horseback. There was a sweet lake of fragrance around her dress that everyone respected. She hadn't paid Kalinko yet. Finally, his turn came. He was tall and lanky: one could say the guy was a wet pair of pants, hanging on a clothesline.

"Kalinko, you come with me," Miss Daniella said. "I need to have some work done in Dad's house."

"But Ma'am…" Kalinko muttered.

"Come with me," she repeated.

"It's Tuesday, Ma'am. It will be Tuesday in the evening, too and…" he started, but Daniella didn't listen to what he had to say.

"I'll pay you in the manor," she said.

That Tuesday evening, Boryana roasted grass snakes, a whole tub of trout, and made a bucketful of tomato salad, although the tomatoes could scarcely be called ripe yet. Tuesday was their Sunday. That Tuesday they collected a lev each and bought a keg of brandy. When October ended, they'd have more money than all the winds in this valley, and they'd go to Pernik. The town of Pernik teemed with girls; the girls in the streets there were more than the paving stones and each girl would love to marry you. When you got married you'd leave 1 lev by her pillow every night, or you could leave her even 2 levs, but you wouldn't tell her why you do that. Of course, you did that because you had got accustomed to it and when you put the money by the clean pillow you'd think for a moment about Boryana. You couldn't forget how beautiful she was.

Meanwhile, no one knew what Daniella was up, so they could only rack their brains trying to riddle out why she wanted that Kalinko guy in the manor. No matter what, the farmhands collected a lev each for the turnip brandy and Boryana made a bucket of green tomato salad for them. That Tuesday they guzzled turnip brandy. The sky turned green with the heat, and the cornfields looked blue, and Boryana was in their heads all the time. No doubt the snakes were to blame for all that. The boys bolted down trout, spat the bones on the grass, and swilled down the turnip brandy.

In the evening Boryana felt blue. Perhaps Daniella had ordered Kalinko to sweep the floors in the manor with the windows all boarded up, or perhaps she'd made him paint the boards white. That Tuesday Boryana chose one guy, then another one, but her sadness was so black that the farmhands collected one more lev each. They gave her the money to buy a necklace when at last the autumn ended. They knew that, like them, she was saving up to get married. Then, she wouldn't charge her man 1 lev the way it was honest and fair, the way she treated them all. She'd roast trout for him, she'd wash his dirty clothes for him, and all weekdays would be Tuesdays for him. That would mean that their life together would be a stream in the valley, their summers would be like the water in the lake, which kept the trout free of charge under its stones. But what would those guys do without Boryana in the wilderness? Yes, one should earn enough money to get married, it was true, but how was it possible to make money if one remained Boryanaless in this scorching heat?

On the following day Kalinko didn't show up. He didn't dig in the cornfields, nor did he weed the pepper gardens. It was not until late in the afternoon when the farmhands noticed a gentleman emerge from the manor house. He wore a suit as white as a trout's belly, his shoes looked as white as trout's eyes, and his Panama hat was as white as trout's gills. Could it be Miss Daniella's fiancé?

"Somebody new is here!" Boryana breathed, spat on her hands, and rubbed at her face to make it clean. "Hey, a nugget of gold comes our way! Let's make him one of us."

The boys reluctantly left the chunks of bread they were chewing. If a guy was up and about since 4 am, watering the tomatoes and peppers, noon would seem as far away as midnight. However, all of them stood up, shouldered their way through the empty crates, and tied their pants with pieces if string. They didn't buy belts, saving up instead to go to Pernik. The girls there were more than the bricks in the walls and all of them were still single. First and foremost, all the girls in Pernik were pretty.

The man in the white suit approached them. As a matter of fact, he ran to them so quickly that the legs of his pants almost ripped along the seams. Right away everybody noticed that the man wasn't Miss Daniella's fiancé. It was Kalinko.

"Kalin, come here!" a booming voice said and they instantly knew who was giving the order: Miss Daniella. "Come back now."

The white sleeves froze in their tracks, the white shoes dug a ditch in the scorched grass, and Kalinko's voice, as small as the gills of a dead trout, wheezed, "Ma'am, may I remain with them, please?"

"No. Come here," Miss Daniella said.

The white hat bowed down, and the white shoes shuffled back to the manor house. The windows, all boarded up, waited.

"What's wrong with him?" the boys wondered.

"Nothing. He's okay. I told her he was the cleanest among you." Boryana explained. "And she knows I untie the ax from my ass when I am with him. She knows Kalinko tells me, 'Let me look at you a minute more'."

"I tell you 'Let me try this side, too'," thundered one of the farmhands, as hefty as the mole in the lake with the trout.

"It's not the same," Boryana cut him short. "Isn't she a bitch?"

"Sometimes she is, but she pays well," the man as strong as the mole pointed out, and he was absolutely right.

The night was thick with skidding bats, the moon shone, a big bottle of brandy in the sky, and there was more moonlight than water in the lake. Suddenly, Boryana waved her ax; she was accustomed to sensing if someone touched her while she was asleep. Perhaps Miss Daniella got all muddled up about what she wanted and had come to take Boryana to her bus with the white dresses.

"Boryana, wake up. It's me."

"I don't work after 2 am," Boryana mumbled, trying to go back to sleep.

"It's me, Kalinko. Boryana, wake up. I still don't have enough money. I even don't have half the money…will you marry me, Boryana?"

"What?"

"Marry me, Boryana. I'll borrow money from you and we'll get married. Later I'll give you everything back…to the last penny. You know I always have."

"Are you sick?" she blurted out, then noticed the moon that lingered on the sky. She knew Kalinko was as meek as clay and one had to encourage him first, so she said softly, "Now tell me what happened."

"Miss Daniella makes me…she makes me tell her what you like. She doesn't believe it's different every time. She said the stars hated her and that she'd go out of her mind."

"Go out of her mind? Why?" Boryana murmured. "She can buy you shoes and different suits for every single day of the week."

"No. She wants to buy you white dresses for every Tuesday in the year. And she wants to visit you on her grandpa's mattress like we do, for 1 lev. I ran away. Marry me and let's beat it. I hope you haven't killed anybody in Pernik."

"No, I haven't. I kicked a guy's ass, that's all."

The wind was as hot as boiling tea and the stars were impatient to meet the month of September in the sky. But September nights were still far away; half a summer of slithering grass snakes and yellow cornfields separated the boys from the money they should make before they caught the bus to the pretty girls in Pernik.

"I don't want a girl from Pernik, Boryana. Wait a minute more. I love looking at you."

The next evening, when the bats were jumping in the hot wind, a woman in a white dress, white hat, and white sandals emerged from the manor house, shouting, "Kalin! Kalin!"

Her sandals hit the dust, her hat wobbled on her head like trout that had just thrown its spawn in the lake, her gorgeous white dress, unbuttoned down to her navel, hung loosely on her.

"Kalin, where are you?"

In fact, the woman knew where Kalinko was, and right away ran to the mattress beside the crates and the empty brandy bottles.

"Boryana, Boryana, get up and come here."

But Boryana didn't show up. She was not there. Miss Daniella established that fact when she lit up the place with her powerful flashlight. The only thing she saw was Boryana's ax, and a couple of grass snakes, left to soak in a bucket of turnip brandy.

"Boryana! Boryana!" the woman shouted so shrilly that some of the workers stirred, although it was too early to go dig in the fields, weed the peppers, or water the tomatoes. "Boryana!"

The farmhands got up and saw Miss Daniella cry, her flashlight illuminating the tears on her face.

"Boryana…" Miss Daniella sobbed. The workers pushed each other, unable to do anything.

"Have a sip of that brandy, Ma'am," suggested the man who was as big as the mole, but she didn't even look at him. Her lips quivered, lisping a sting of quiet words, as if she was thirsty and couldn't reach the moonlit lake.

After two weeks the workers left the house which Miss Daniella's grandfather had built. They took their money on the 17th of August, and on the following day when Miss Daniella, forgetting to put on her white dress, rode Balzac and checked the fields, she saw that the house was empty. Two broken crates, several empty beer bottles, and a grass snake's hide were left near the torn mattress. Perhaps Miss Daniella wasn't aware that even if a guy ate green tomato salad four times a day, Boryana was in his mind all the time, and Boryana was in his eyes, too.

Tuesday became more important than Sunday. Tuesday would not come to the manor house if Boryana wasn't there.

Miss Daniella knew that for sure.

Schatzi, My Treasure

"Schatzi! Schatzi!" the woman shouted at the top of her voice as the scraggy dog stood in the middle of the small square trembling, his thin legs glistening in the semidarkness.

It was a small mongrel. The woman appeared as scraggy as her little beast though not as old as him. "Schatzi!" she called out once again but the dog didn't budge. The little square was well lit. There were cars parked everywhere and it was raining. The woman looked around and stood hesitant, finally silent. The small dog glanced at her, expecting a sign, her shrill voice or a wave of her hand maybe, but she didn't do anything. She rushed to the shadow of the neat, clean block of flats, thick gray dusk that was alive with murmurs of a TV, stifled talks of the tenants, and darkness.

"Hey!" a man called out sharply from the shadow.

"Are you there?" the woman whispered and rushed towards the voice. The dog trotted behind her, its tail trembling. The man didn't say anything, and she couldn't see him, but she stumbled on, the twilight enveloping her and her meager dog.

"Here," the rough voice called out. The woman still couldn't see anybody and ran towards his voice.

"I missed you," she said to the darkness. The nice block of flats went on spewing TV newscasts at the woman's shadow. "I missed you, Franz," she repeated after she finally found him. Franz let her kiss him on the chin then allowed her to kiss the wet collar of his sweatshirt.

"Have you brought money?" he asked staying still, his hands in his pockets.

"Yes. Yes," she muttered, pressing against him. The scraggy dog whimpered at his mistress's feet but the woman paid no attention to it. It tried to rub its back against her boots but she ignored its presence.

"Let me see," said the man. The woman fumbled in her pocket and produced a couple of bills that quickly got wet in her small hand. The man grabbed the money and took a few steps towards the narrow square with the rows of cars parked in the puddle of light under the streetlamps. He was a big man in a denim coat and blue jeans, almost twice as big as the woman. He counted the money and threw the banknotes on the wet asphalt.

"That's not enough," he said and started to go.

"Wait, Franz," she pleaded, her voice another puddle of rain in the cold square. "Wait please," she dug in her pockets, her hands impatient, hurrying, panicking. She produced a handful of coins and reached out to him. "Here, Franz. Take that, too."

The man took his time counting the coins. His lips moved silently as his fingers rubbed the rain off the cents.

"Okay," he said at last. The woman heaved a happy sigh, took hold of his hand, then tentatively, furtively kissed his wet leather jacket, waiting for his reaction. The man didn't object and she plucked up courage. Her lips climbed up his neck slowly, cold thin lips that had shouted so desperately for the dog a minute ago. The man didn't move. His hands were still in his pockets. She was too short and her lips couldn't reach his mouth. The dog was too near her boots. Perhaps she had stepped on his tiny paw for it gave out a short shrill wail.

The man was annoyed. He tried to kick it but his foot missed its soft fur.

"No, no. Don't do that Franz," the woman said. "He's a good thing."

The man didn't listen. He kicked again and missed.

"Give me the dog," he said.

"No, Franz, no," she pleaded. "Let's go to my place. Please."

The dog padded to the shadow of the cars and stayed in the dark, a little piece of wet night which could breathe and bark.

"I don't want to go to your place," he said. "There's a bench. Come here."

"But it's wet. It's cold," she said shivering.

"Then take back your money and beat it," he said. "Don't waste my time."

"No. No, Franz. Please, no. Let me stay."

The man made a rapid motion with his leg. This time his boot caught the scraggy back of the mutt. A sharp whimper hit the cars parked nearby.

"Schatzi!" the woman whimpered too.

In the light of the streetlamps the couple of wrinkles on her face appeared deeper in spite of the rouge she had

used. The man's face was unshaven; his rugged features
had young cruel beauty about them that made him con-
spicuous even in that narrow square. In the distance the
electric train to the Hauptbahnhoff, the main railway station in Aachen, cut the evening into two parts – the Alte
Stadt, the Old Town, with St. Mary Cathedral where tourists thronged day and night, and the part of Nopius Street
to which Schatzi, whose name in English meant 'treasure',
the clean narrow squares and clean wet benches belonged.

Franz turned to go but the woman ran after him and
grabbed his hand. A little ball of wet fur and panting
scrawny muzzle trotted in her wake. Schatzi.

"Okay, Okay Franz," she blurted out. "Let's go to the
bench."

He slowly turned round and plodded back to the naked
wall of the neat block of flats and its thick shadow. The
woman caught up with him and reached for his hand. He
didn't pull it. She caught his palm between her hands and
pressed it hard. Franz turned away from her, but sat on the
bench all the same. It was raining and it was very cold. He sat
immobile, his back rigidly upright, his hands on his knees.

"I love you, Franz," she said and kissed the sleeves of
his jacket, then she kissed the copper buttons and his jeans,
and she kissed his immobile neck and she kissed his stubbly chin. Then she slowly, hesitantly, kissed his hair. It
rained but not very hard, a fine obstinate drizzle that
squeezed its way through the dead leaves of the autumn
and stuck to the cars parked under the light of the streetlamps. She tried to kiss his mouth but he didn't let her. His

body was firm, unyielding, and hard. She admired it. She loved it. If only he would let her love him a minute more, a couple of seconds more, a heartbeat more. The dog was a thick piece of the night mingled with shaggy fur. His heart in his little muzzle, he stood by that wet cold bench watching the woman kiss the boot that had kicked him in the ribs. The puny beast stared rigid beyond itself with fear. That boot could kick his mistress. And his mistress gave him food, and she gave him her soft good hands to rub his nose against.

"I love you, Franz," the woman whispered. Franz didn't say anything. His strong muscular body pushed and beat into hers, rhythmically, like a powerful turbine. Suddenly the turbine stopped churning and he pushed her aside.

"Franz," she whispered. "Franz, it was magnificent."

He stood up, abrupt and big, a hulking mass which thickened the darkness. It was still drizzling and a wind blew, a thin and cutting gust of freezing air the dog could never get accustomed to. In Aachen wind and rain went together like a pair of twins. The narrow square tingled and the national German flags fluttered, tied to their poles in front of the buildings. The last train rolled along its rails to the more dazzling half of the town where the magnificent cathedral Aachener Dom waited for the admiration of the tourists. Here, nearby the small square, Nopius Strasse waited, dissolving in the wind. That was the only street Schatzi knew in Aachen, and that was the only bench in the neighborhood which the dog hated. Maybe he didn't even hate it, for a little treasure like him could hardly hate.

That bench was simply a big lump under his ribs and it was always there when his nose smelled the wet stench of that man's jeans and his mistress's kisses on them. It was simply that thin treacherous wind again. It broke umbrellas and it broke his animal heart. In the autumn, it stole from the dogs the soft caring hands of the women who gave their pets everything they had.

"Don't go, Franz," the woman said and Schatzi felt a big lump in his mouth. When the voice of his mistress was that flat and gray, the lump that stuck in Schatzi's heart almost suffocated him. The man didn't say anything. His steps thudded heavily, big sharp steps like knives cutting through bones.

"Will you come next Tuesday, Franz?"

Suddenly the man stopped.

"It depends," he said.

"It depends?" she repeated hopefully the night suddenly cozy and quiet in her voice. "It depends on what?"

"Bring me the dog," he said.

"Schatzi! Schatzi!" the woman called out. "Come here, Schatzi" She caught the wet ball of fur in which drizzle and stars were mixed, and caressed the small prickling ears. "Schatzi," she whispered reassuringly. Then she looked at the man. "The dog…" she started. "The dog….what will you …you won't …."

The man took the furry bundle of bones and squeezed it. A short wail erupted between the fists of the man. Then it abruptly died. Franz lifted the dog above his head and let it drop onto the black wet asphalt. There was another wail, longer than the one before.

"Schatzi!" the woman sobbed. "Schatzi!"

"I'll let you do it again," Franz said and sat back on the bench. The woman slumped by his side, sobbing.

"Shut up," Franz said. "If you don't shut up I won't come on Tuesday."

She tried hard to stop sobbing and she kissed his neck.

Suddenly the narrow square was quiet. The night train to the Bahnhoff was gone. Then Schatzi wailed once again but dogs did that often, didn't they? Wailing was a natural part of a dog's life.

GRANITE

Shon didn't have enough money. All his friends had forgotten him. He couldn't pay his sex tax and that meant that he could no longer be a man. He'd be processed into a stone, and he knew he'd be deaf and blind dust. Each particle of the dust he would turn into would be listening to her steps. Eya. How could he forget her? He'd been a stone several times for her.

Her family would never agree to pay his sex tax. They didn't want him around; they were heaps of brown stones around her and he had to climb and crawl to surmount them. He had to endure in order to reach her. They were endless hard sharp crags closing in on him, encircling Eya. When finally he managed to pay his tax her father told him she had been processed into sand or a heap of stones. Shon went looking for her. How could he be sure she was the gray rock jutting like a knife into the sky? He believed he'd know, he'd been dust, lowly powder without form of its own, and he'd been a rock, so he knew: a rock would recognize if another rock was Eya.

She used to be a small island lost in the see, then she was a dune. She was a hillock of sand and he was the wind in the night that touched it gently, very carefully. He loved her so much he wanted to be dust all his days without her.

Shon had been sandstone and granite. He'd been patient. He'd been mud.

And he had been a digger for years and years. Diggers were the sexless workers who cut the stones and carried the bags of sand with which other diggers built houses. He had been a stone and a bag of sand and other diggers had built a house with him. He mixed with other stones and he couldn't pay his sex tax to become a man. He had remained a wall of a house forever, rubble in the base of a mausoleum, a tile on its roof, a chimney dead with smoke. He could not become a man until the house crumbled, until the roof disintegrated and the chimney melted away.

The diggers were losers, the despicable riff-raff that lived to grab money. They were happy when they stole small change or killed other diggers for small change. They were no men or women; they were bad eggs that had no embryos in them. After ages of building houses and making roads they could finally pay to be men or women for a day. Shon knew very well what it felt like to be a digger. He had built a garden amidst a desert for a newlywed couple. He watched as they kissed and he was there while they made love. His task was to bring them water and food. They liked his docility and paid him well.

Even while he was a digger he never forgot. He didn't know where Eya was. He hoped she was not a digger like him. He hoped he could earn enough to buy her off, to pay her sex tax. Her parents could pay any price and she could remain a girl all her life. Her parents could find a different man for her every time she was a woman, but

Eya…

Shon remembered…

"You are my bread and you are my hunger," she had said. "I don't want anybody else. I'd rather be a digger all my life…or a house that will never collapse if you are not with me."

Shon didn't want any other girl. He could afford to be a man an hour every year. There would be women for him. He could find a sweetheart and she'd love him; being a woman was a short-lived bliss and every second was a treasure. It was a common sight to see a man caressing a peace of stone: his woman had no more money to pay her sex tax and her time as a girl had passed. Sometimes a woman held a pebble in her hand; that was the man she had kissed a minute before.

Shon knew what happened after the kiss. Women threw the pebbles away and rushed to find other men. Every second counted. Every heartbeat was a reward. Men got rid of the stones that had been the love of their days. No one wasted time.

Eya was in his dreams. On the day he was a man, one short winter day in the endless year, he didn't look for another girl. He wanted Eya. 'You are my shore and my infinity,' Eya had said. Eya, his Eya.

"He's sick," the diggers said. "He's deranged. He's a stone that has crumbled the wrong way."

But Shon was not a stone that had crumbled the wrong way. He hoped Eya was a pebble he could press to his heart.

"I'll pay the digger to carve your name on me, after he

processes me into a stone, Shon," she had said. "And you'll know where I am. You'll find me."

"Your parents won't let you be a stone. They'll find someone for you."

"No," she said. "I will not be a woman for anybody else!"

He could not find her.

He'd been an outcrop of granite for all eternity before he made enough money to become a man again. He paid a digger to carve her name on the gray rough rock he had turned into. It cost him all he had earned while he was sand, and what he had saved up while he was dust and mud. The digger that had carved Eya's name on him could afford to remain a man for an interminable week on Shon's money.

Shon waited. He was a granite block. Winds hit him and the mist slept on him making his surface slippery and freezing cold. Birds perched on him and moss grew on him, destroying his crystals. Shon made money by slowly dying. He hoped the moss had not covered Eya's name. He prayed it remained cut deep and sharp into him.

One day Eya came. She touched the moss that grew on his surface. She dug carefully, very slowly the mist that enveloped him. She cleared the leaves of the trees that had been falling onto him for years.

"Shon," she said. "Dearest Shon!"

A stone cannot feel, Schon had been told that many times. A stone is dead. A stone cannot love the summers and the winds. Shon knew all that. But that was not true. There she was, his Eya.

You are my bread and my hunger. You are my eyes.

You are my mist, and my birds, Eya.

He understood her words. He could feel her touch. He had been a sexless digger so long, and he had loved her. He had been dust, the storms had scattered him all over the world, and he'd loved her. He had been a road of stones that her parents destroyed, and he'd loved her.

…Something was happening. His surface broke. Deep crevices cut through his cold depth, the moss which grew on him caught fire. He had paid that digger to carve Eya's name on him. Now, her name was no more. His crystals creaked and shrieked, his granite depth writhed and shook. There was no more strength in him. He was not a stone any more. He was not sand, not even dust. He didn't know what was happening to him.

Then he heard her voice.

"Look!"

"Yes, you were right, my child."

That was her father speaking. Shon could understand. He recognized the man by his firm touch. Shon had been a stone and her father had kicked him and pushed him hundreds of times.

"Look at it. What a beautiful ruby!" another voice said, of a man Shon had never seen before. "You wouldn't imagine cheap granite could make such a splendid ruby!"

"Oh, they all do, James," her father said. "The trick is to make them fall in love."

"My fiancée is very good at that," said the man Shon had never seen. "You are unbelievable, Eya. Congratulations."

"Thank you, James."

There were no winds and no mist. Shon was not a man and had no heart. Something much more powerful than a heart broke in him.

"Let's wrench that beautiful ruby from this rubbish heap," her father said.

"That's the best gem in your collection, dear," the man she called James remarked as he carefully placed Shon in a box. A dozen of other smaller rubies sparkled momentarily under the thick lid.

You are my bread and my hunger. You are my coast and my infinity, the thing that was more powerful than a heart screamed deep inside Shon.

Perhaps Eya didn't know that a ruby was a stone that would live longer than the wind.

MUSIC FOR MY SON
For my friend Afshan from Afghanistan

"They say you've got an ear for music. It's nothing important, of course," Atash said. "But I want to know how it happens. How you catch it, that damned music of yours. Tell me."

I told him nothing.

When I saw an oak tree I could hear its roots bite the dry stones, fighting for water. There was sand and rubble in the valley all around us, and there was only one well. It rained so rarely I forgot what rain looked like.

My voice was no good, too weak to speak about the heat at night and the blazing sun at noon. There was a cave that the winds had carved in the sandstone. I hid in it and I hummed or I wailed. I chanted in the dark, and there were no words in my song. I was afraid to hum outside the cave. My father would say I was crazy, my brothers would say I had a screw loose.

"What are you singing about, son?" My mother asked one evening. "Days are bitter and there is nothing to sing about. You'd better learn quick. Your father wants a blacksmith in the family and you are strong." Then she ruffled my hair and said, "You sing beautifully, son."

"Nonsense woman," dad said. "He's got to work. No

singing. It's a waste of time."

So I had to hide in that cave and I wailed in the night. Then hunger in my belly was bigger than the dry sky. Dad brawled at me, my brothers learned quickly. I didn't. And there was that girl, Afshan who sneaked to the cave.

"What are you doing here?" I said. "Spying on me?"

"I'm listening to you," she said.

"You are crazy," I said. "Go away. Go away or I'll break your neck." She went away.

One night my mother came to the cave.

"Shan," she said. "Where did you hear that song?"

"It's not a song," I said. "It doesn't have anything in it, just a tune poor like us."

"It's huge," she said. "That tune is richer than a bag full of money."

I didn't tell mother the song was about her as well. It was a hole in our backyard and there was no water in it. The heat had drained the moisture at the bottom and dad was angry he had to dig deeper. But even deeper there was no water and dad was mad.

A tiny part in the tune I hummed was about the girl who wanted to listen to me, the one I'd driven away.

"Humming and wailing doesn't fill an empty belly," dad said to mom. "He must be a blacksmith. He is a lousy learner and I don't like that."

"I have three brothers," I said. "Let them become blacksmiths."

"You eat my bread and my cheese and you'll be a blacksmith."

"He sings well," my mother said. "He sings tunes no one has heard."

"Shut up, woman. There is no voice in his mouth worth speaking about," dad said.

I knew that.

That winter the snow was waist-deep and I was lucky dad dragged me to Atash's smithy. It was a wonderful place. I worked in the dark and I roared at the top of my lungs. No one could hear me. At times, Afshan sneaked to the narrow square in front of the smithy, but she didn't dare to enter the workshop. She stood by the door for a minute and I roared on hoping she could hear me.

It was Afshan who brought Atash to the workshop. She didn't dare to cross the threshold and I was sorry for her.

"This is Shan who can sing, sir," she said and ran away.

Atash was a small dark man. He wore a leather coat and good boots.

"Afshan says you sing," the man said. "Sing to me."

I didn't like his voice.

"Why should I sing to you?" I said looking at his good boots. I knew he was a rich guy but I didn't like even his good boots.

"I'll give you two tans," the man said.

Two tans! A stove, a packet of coffee and a bag of potatoes cost two tans.

"Sing!" Atash said.

I bent down and tapped on the cauldron I was working on, feeling the weight of my hammer all over me. The man took a bundle out of his pocket and waved it under my nose.

I went on hitting the big black cauldron in which soup for a whole village could be cooked.

"Don't waste my time," Atash said.

I hummed under my breath. I tried hard not to look at him.

I saw the cave I loved and I remembered the well that had run dry. I thought of the big cauldron and I saw the village waiting for that rich soup. I knew the children hoped to get a piece of the cooked goat, and I saw their mothers praying there would be enough for everybody. I saw my mother, too, and I saw Afshan. There was nothing left in the cauldron for Afshan, and there were no words for the song I wanted.

"You don't want the two tans," Atash said.

I wanted the money but my mother was not around me any more. I didn't see the snow in the street and I couldn't hear the wind. I forgot about the cauldron for the rich soup. I watched the man's coat but I didn't envy him. I hummed and I choked on the air, then I hummed on.

"Who taught you these tunes?"

"These are no tunes," I said.

The man was silent. I went on hammering the cauldron.

It had started snowing, the fire glowed in front of me and it was hot in the workshop. Atash's boots sparkled and his face shone red. The cauldron was almost ready.

"You make music for me and I feed you and your brothers," Atash said.

I went on hammering the cauldron.

"Your brothers are hungry," he went on. I worked with

my hammer trying not to think of my brothers and of our backyard with the dry hole of the well in it. "Your mother's hungry," he whispered.

I saw the trough in the cellar scraped empty, and I thought of the hen-coop behind our house with no hens in it. I saw my mother limping down the fields to pluck some nettles and cook soup for us.

"I'll make music for you," I said.

It was snowing hard outside. I looked at Atash's red face and I thought I couldn't stand the heat in the room.

"You make music for me the way I tell you," he said buttoning up his coat "Or I'll kick you out."

I wondered if Afshan was somewhere near the door. Maybe she'd heard what Atash told me.

----------- ----------- --------

"There'll be no lunch for you today," Mr. Atash said. "You were not diligent enough."

He'd given me an old clarinet, dented and scratched, and said, "Play."

"I don't know how."

He showed me and said, "Play. You play four hours what I've showed you. Don't stop."

It was a simple tune, dry and flat. I repeated it a couple of times and I tried a different thing.

It was then that he'd said for the first time, "There'll be no lunch for you. You were not diligent enough."

There were many days with no lunch for me.

At the end of the winter, he showed me the notes. They were little black dots that meant sounds. I'd heard before

148

there was a way of putting music to paper and make even deaf men hear it. In the beginning, the notes looked dead to me, sprawling like dead lice on the white sheet of paper. Then I discovered a thing I'd never believed: the paper could sing. The notes made the old clarinet new, but that was nothing, they could make the rain stop falling. They killed the hunger in my belly.

Mr. Atash gave me two sheets of paper with notes on them and said "Play this for three hours."

I played the piece for twenty minutes then I jotted down new notes. They were black dots of sounds that were big sandy valleys stretching as long as my eyes hurt. They tasted of the thorns I collected for my mother to make tea for us in the cold evenings. They were the cool dark caves in summer, they were biting winds, and they were the wolves in winter, too. The wolves were starving, and the notes I wrote on the paper were dangerous and evil.

"You didn't play what I ordered you," Atash said. "You were not diligent enough. There will be no lunch and no dinner for you."

I didn't care. I remained in the dark corridor where my bed was and played the clarinet. I loved every dent in it. I'd kissed its every scratch. Hunger was in my belly, but I had the clarinet. I had the summers and the blazing sun, and I had the snowdrifts and the wolves. I didn't mind it was freezing cold in the corridor where I slept. The walls were covered with drops of water and there was no window at my place.

"You don't play what I order you to," Atash said to me.

"You are not diligent enough." He saw that I could survive without dinners and he added, "You don't listen to me. There'll be no fire in the corridor where you live."

The drops of water on the walls froze. I had my clarinet and I saw the enormous sand dunes and the scorching sun on them. I played and the valleys came to me. I wished Afshan knew I made summers for her, and I left warm pebbles in the tunes because I hoped she liked them.

Then one day Atash said, "You are not diligent enough. Give me the clarinet."

He took it and I remained in the windowless corridor, with the hunger in my belly and the frozen drops on the walls. I wished Afshan was here. I could hum to her and she'd know I was trying to make another summer day for her. I wished my mother were here. She always had a chunk of bread hidden for me. You sing beautifully Shan, she'd say. I didn't have my clarinet and I tried to remember the time when my mother and I sang together. She never had enough time, she had to cook for my father and my brothers, and she had to wash our clothes. She didn't have a beautiful voice. Her voice was weak, but the words she said were beautiful. She sang slowly like a lonely bird with a broken wing in the autumn, not strong enough to follow the flock. My mother sang rarely but then the time stopped. Her song was a wind that brought rain to our house and it was a soft shadow of a smile. I wished mother was here. I'd only tell her I was OK and then I'd let her go to cook for father and for my brothers. Without her, our house would be like me without my clarinet.

At a certain point, I found a way out. I started putting the black dots of the notes on every piece of paper I laid my hands on. I was hungry and the walls reeled before my eyes. I tried to eat some snow, and I thought that perhaps my father was right. I should have learned to be a blacksmith; a blacksmith's belly was full almost all the time. Hunger and cold made me wail. It must have been horrible that wailing of mine. I wanted to escape from the corridor, but Atash had locked the door. I screamed about Afshan, about my clarinet. I screamed until I had no more power to open my mouth.

I heard people clapping their hands. "Go on, Shan, go on."

Those were the other boys from Atash's smithy, four altogether.

"Eat," a voice shouted. I recognized it. Atash, my master, stood at the other end of the corridor. I remembered he also played the clarinet and for once I was sorry for him. He played it so poorly as if all his teeth hurt him at one at the same time and his clarinet was full of worms. He threw me a chunk of bread.

"Where did you learn that song you've just hummed?" Atash asked.

"It's not a song," I said guzzling the bread.

"It was a beautiful piece," he said. "Is it about that girl Afshan who has forgotten all about you?"

"It's about that girl Afshan who hasn't forgotten me," I said.

That night Atash came to the corridor where my bed

was. There were icicles on the walls. I had eaten goat's tallow to keep warm. The blankets were not enough, I had put on all my clothes and I had crept under the mattress with my boots on.

"Take the clarinet," Atash said kicking the side of my bed. "Play!"

He waved the clarinet above my head, a dented, scratched piece, pitted and lusterless.

"Play that song you were screaming. Play and I will let you eat a whole roasted rabbit if I like the tune."

I didn't remember anything about screaming a song. That was the hunger in my belly and the thought my mother had to bring water from the frozen river. I knew her old torn shoes and her frozen feet. I sang no song, no I didn't. That was the despair I had not seen Afshan.

My clarinet was in my hands, and the thing had a beau-u-tiful voice. I didn't play on it about Afshan although I wanted to so much. I didn't play about my mother and her poky fireplace; I didn't play about the nasty wind and the snowdrifts that were bigger than my courage. I played about the rabbit, about how he jumped in the warm sum-mer and how they killed him, and how much I wanted to grab the grilled meat, gnaw at the bones, guzzle the sauce, eat everything to the last tiny morsel, lick the platter clean, gulp down the last drop of grease on it. The old clarinet was hungry with me, and its dents and scratches were an endless day in summer, so hot that the icicles on the walls all melted down.

Atash was gaping at me.

"Stop! Stop!" he shouted. "I'll bring you the roasted rabbit."

He let me eat it all. It was a huge rabbit, as big as a mountain. I ate and I ate and ate, and my stomach ached, but I could not stop. I crushed the bones and sucked the marrow from them then I gnawed at the squashed pieces and swallowed them. They were so delicious.

Atash looked at me and said, "Give me your right hand."

I stretched it out and he took it. He stared at my fingers then he bent and caught hold of the ax. I used it when I chopped the firewood I dragged out from the dilapidated shed.

Atash looked very calm and relaxed.

"You think you are a good musician," he said.

Suddenly he lifted the ax and let it drop onto my right hand. Blood spurted out. He hit me again. He hit my hand hard.

It hurt. I thought I was dying. There was blood on the floor and there was blood on his trousers.

"You are the devil," Atash said. "It is impossible for a human being to play like that."

It hurt. My old clarinet, dented and battered, lay on the floor, in a pool of blood.

One of the boys came with a wash basin.

"It will heal, Shan," he muttered. "Atash had to kill the devil, you know."

He washed the blood and poured brandy onto the wound.

"I wish I had a devil like yours in me," he said. "I'll

have to throw you out, Shan. Atash ordered me to. Will you forgive me?"

My hand hurt and I was dizzy. I didn't know if I lay on the snow or I was on the clouds that were mixed with the wind.

I saw red drops on the road. I saw my mother's face above me and I saw Afshan's face. I knew they were not there but I kept on looking at them.

"Afshan will marry me," Atash said. "She will. Then perhaps I'll be able to make music like you."

My hand didn't heal well enough to hold a hammer. It could not hold a clarinet either. The sand valleys remained there, my mother's fireplace was there, in my smashed hand. The winter was there and I gave it to the paper with my music. I gave the paper scorching August sun and freezing rains, I gave it the sky full of cold moons. I gave it my mother's soft voice when she sang and the time stopped to wait for her. I gave it Afshan's smile that was always there. Afshan didn't leave my music for a second.

All tunes I made were for Afshan who did not become Atash's wife. I could never stop making them for her.

"You couldn't become a blacksmith," she said. "So what? Don't you worry. Don't worry you can't play the clarinet. You make music and your music is strong. I want to listen to it. I want to listen to you to the last day of my life."

And the black notes, as tiny as lentil grains, became bigger than the hills, became quiet and soft, like the old broken clarinet I could hold no more.

But I filled the summer with the most beautiful music, the lullaby Afshan sang to my son.

CLANS
For Omari from Afghanistan

You shouldn't have done it, Boosa.

Happiness is a simple thing, you said. Happiness is a cool shadow and you looking at me. But we don't have cool shadows in Trun. In summer there is no grass. The dust is knee-deep and it is so hot your heels bleed, and there are flies in the thick air that drink water from your eyes. The sun is so red you can't look at it. There are no trees. I will not be in Trun to look any more, Boosa. Yesterday Farzin came to my father. They talked for a while. You know what happens when Farzin comes to a guy's shack. My mother cried when Farzin went out and dad didn't look me in the eyes.

"Babur," he said. "They'll come to take you tomorrow. You can go to say goodbye to your brothers." Then dad smoked and his eyes were in the dust as he said, "Farzin said he'd bring you back to us. They won't cut your face, he said."

Mom was silent. She wiped her eyes with the back of her hand, then she went behind the shack. You never saw her blubber or cry. She came back carrying our old goat, she had killed it and there was blood on her hands. It would've been better if dad scolded her. What would the other kids eat now, that was what he should have said. Dad said nothing. My brothers were all looking at me, saying nothing. My sisters were there saying nothing.

"I'll cook a stew for you, son," Mom said pressing the dead goat to her puny chest.

A week ago after the sand storm, one of the shepherds found a dead man. That man's throat was slashed. He was from the Hamasa clan and his body was strong. I knew this man—he used to collect dry thorns for his goats in the mountain.

Happiness is a simple thing, you said: daylight and you looking at me. If one of the Hamasa men got killed, one of our Feda men had to be killed. Blood for blood, it was as simple as that.

"Housyar, you'd better decide which of yours will be the one," Farzin had said to dad. "I'll come to collect him after midday bread. He has to be the same age as the dead Hamasa guy. They don't want an old man and they don't want a sick man. You know what will happen if you don't give one of yours."

Mom knew what would happen. The Hamasas would come and kill my seven brothers one by one. They wouldn't kill my sisters. There were worse things one could do to a woman, things worse than death. There were too many mouths that wanted to eat in that mountain. And there was dust, knee-deep, hot brown powder, in which thorns grew. But thorns were not enough. There were goats that ate them and water was too scarce to grow more. No court and no law came to Trun. No one had ever seen a judge. Farzin would come to take a new guy after midday bread. Two days later, Farzin would drive the body back to his family. The guy's brothers and sisters would wash him, and in the evening when it was not so hot, they drank tea. The Hamasas like us, made tea from the thorns. It was bitter. It made you dizzy, you saw things that were not there, but you slept. You slept like a stone, and you didn't see the body of your dead brother.

"Babur," Dad said to me, "You are the weakest. This way, or the other you won't live long. But don't you show the Hamasas you are sick, my son. Go pick the thorns. Let the Hamasas see you picking them."

You know there's something wrong in my chest, Boosa. You've seen me cough and wheeze. If I go out when it rains, I choke on the wind. I fall and I pray the rain turns into a drizzle. I can't walk.

Dad was right. This way or the other, I wouldn't last long. But, Boosa, you know happiness is a simple thing. Some wind, some thorns for our tea, and you. If I weren't sick, they wouldn't let me come to your shack, would they?

"Babur is a sick wreck," your mother said. "And he's got a good mouth. He thinks up good tales. There's no harm listening to him."

Then I learned happiness was a simple thing. "Got another of your sweet lies, Babur?" your mother would say. I didn't, but the dust was full of summer tales, and there were thorns boiling for tea. And in winter, there was snow taller than the shacks, and there were thorns again, burning in the hearth. Maybe I was to blame for everything. I taught you to believe in the nonsense I spoke to you and your sisters.

You shouldn't have done that, Boosa.

Midday passed, and the stew Mom made with the goat she'd killed waited on the table. I asked myself what the other kids would eat later. There was no milk for the new baby and no meat for the sick. My brothers looked at me. They didn't eat. Dad and Mom didn't eat either. My sisters looked at me, the youngest one sobbing softly, the others quiet. I thought about the fairytales. Snow was bread, Mom had told me, and dust was flour. The best flour you could find in Trun Mountain.

"No crying," Dad said. "Eat."

We waited.

"Run away," Mom had said to me the night before. "We can bring you something to eat."

"He's sick," Dad's voice crawled like the dust. "They'll kill him and they'll kill us. Better eat the stew she cooked for you, son."

We waited and waited and Farzin didn't come.

"What does he want?" Dad grumbled. "Perhaps he expects us to bring you to him?" No way, that had never happened before. No man in his right mind would do such a cowardly thing. I tried not to think about it, Boosa. I remembered when it rained. Not during the downpour, when the valley was a cauldron of steaming red mud and black clouds, but about the flowers that sprouted after the rain. Red and blue and yellow, they grew on the roofs of the shacks and they shot up under our feet, so many that we couldn't see the sand.

"Babur," you said. "These flowers are just like the tales you told us. Look at them. Happiness is a simple thing."

If I hadn't been sick your father wouldn't have let me talk to you. Your mother wouldn't bring tea for me. And I told you a lie once, Boosa.

"Take a handful of the wet mud after the rain is over and knead it well. Put some petals of the flowers in that mud and let it dry. Then give that ball of dry clay to the person you want to be happy. And he will be." It was a lie, Boosa. I found a ball of dry clay in front of our shack. My sisters told me you made it for me.

"I'll go instead of you, Babur," Dad said.

We all knew it was impossible. The dead Hamasa guy was strong and young. Dad was old. I was the weakest man in the whole village and the cold in the winter would take me soon, or the heat in summer would.

"But nobody can tell such beautiful tales, Babur," you said. "You know what the dust speaks and you know what the wolves think. And you know where the flowers go after the rain is over."

"Chew this when they start beating you," Dad said. "Chew and it won't hurt."

"Babur, run away, son! I won't give you to them!"

"But the village has made a decision, woman," Dad said.

"We'll run away from the village."

"Then our own clan will catch us. Your own brothers will stone you to death, woman."

"I don't care. I won't give them Babur."

"If they don't kill me, Mom, I won't make it through the winter."

"You'll make it, son, you'll make it. You can take my word for it. Run, Babur!"

Then Dad went up to her, he walked very slowly to her, as he always did. He went slowly up to her and hit her.

"Say one more word and I kill you," he told her.

"Kill me," she said. "Kill me. I won't give them Babur."

Dad's hand went limp. No one ate from the goat stew and the shack was full of the most beautiful aroma the mountain had ever seen. My sisters were quiet. The midday eating had to be over. I knew it by the shadows of the peaks, which crept on the ground and mixed with the dust. Farzin came in. No one had heard him drag his feet on the gravel. He dragged his feet and kicked the dust when he came to collect our guy for the Hamasas. He had killed more people than there were stones in the village now.

"Babur can stay with you," he said slowly. "Now give me a bowl of your stew for the good news I brought you."

Ma gave out a sob. My brothers stood up.

"Don't make fun of me," Dad wheezed. "You are an important man, but it's my house."

"Keep your sickly son of yours at home," Farzin said. "Somebody else went to the Hamasas instead of him."

The silence was thicker than the heat. Dad's face was gray, Mom's cracked lips bled.

"Give me that stew," Farzin said.

"Who went instead of him?" Dad croaked.

"You wouldn't want to know."

"Tell me who went instead of him, and I'll give you some stew."

Farzin's face sweated, his lips were wet with saliva. He swallowed a couple of times.

"Boosa went instead of him," Farzin said. "Ran away from her family. Her father, old Giti, cropped his hair. Shame on them! That girl must have been mad. The whole family is disgraced."

I could not hear Farzin talk. I saw you picking the flowers after that big rain, and I saw you make a big heart of clay with the flower petals in it.

"You'll be healthy, Babur," you said.

Boosa, why did you do that! I can no longer see the dust, and I cannot see the mountain. I see what they are doing to you. I wish you were dead. I wish I were dead.

"Boosa is young and strong," Farzin said.

"She won't die quickly," Dad said.

"She's young and she'll last long," Farzin said. "Each one of the Hamasa lads will have a piece of her as long as she lasts."

I hit Farzin as hard as I could. I hit him, and I hit him and I hit him as long as I could see him. Then there was dust in my mouth and blood in my eyes.

Boosa, I see you in the evening when the sky sleeps. I see you in the daylight. Happiness is a simple thing.

In the heat it suddenly rained. Clouds and skies and dust mingled and the valley was a lake of red mud and stones. Goats were drowned in the whirlpools. And then the sun shone. There were flowers—red and blue and yellow and lilac, all the mountain was flowers.

I'll come and find you, Boosa. I'll come to the Hamasas and I'll find you. And I will tell you the most beautiful tale. Happiness is a simple thing. Happiness is you.

CARTS

We are all strong and difficult people in our family. My father drank, it was true, but he made the best cornel brandy in Southern Bulgaria, and Bulgarians, Jews, and Greeks alike gave their last pennies to buy Dad's home brew for their sons' weddings. My elder brother was the best rider in the country far and wide, and my younger brother could drink as much as all eels in the Struma River without falling from his chair. My sister sang beautifully. Guys gave her jars of honey and covered the path to our small house with roses for her to step on.

My mother wove woolen rugs and she could cure fidgety children who scared easily. She cast lead bullets for them, and while the lead melted in the pot she mumbled the kid's name under her breath. Then the little one forgot all his fright and fears. I'd seen this time and again. I couldn't explain what happened, not if my life depended on it. Mother was held in high esteem and Dad was a man to be reckoned with. I was the only person who lacked distinction.

That was bad.

I cared for Grisha.

I had noticed Grisha first when Dad organized the Big Bet. To be honest, he didn't organize anything, he let our neighbors drink some of his cornel thunder and that was enough. Guys could hardly pay him for the brandy they'd imbibed. It was true Grisha repaired his motorbike for free, another guy dug our cornfield for Mother, a cousin of ours plastered the walls of our living room. The guys had carts and good horses, Dad made wonderful brandy but no one could pay him well enough.

The Big Bet was a race in which the best cart and the best horse won. Grisha was a magician because he made your horse-drawn vehicle glitter, sing and sparkle. The competitors climbed in their carts and raced down the dirt road, stirring up dust as black as midnight, hooves hitting stones and crushing them into powder. The guy who won didn't collect money, for there was no money among the cornel brandy drinkers. As clever as he was, Dad thought up an interesting reward for the champion in the Big Bet. The winner chose one man among the population of the village to work for him for a day without being paid. It was very easy to guess who the most sought-after guy was: Grisha.

Grisha was the only man in the district who could make your old Volkswagen start in the dead of winter. His shoulders were as broad as the dirt road that clambered the hill to our place. I loved the way he spoke, slowly and powerfully like a church bell.

Our village was big, all green and warm at the end of summer, and the river had not run dry completely. Some big shots from the nearby town drove their old Fords and Peugeots, pushed them into the gorge the river had dug, and left them there, in the thick mud, to rot away. But they didn't know Grisha! He fixed the jalopies. From three rotten Fords, he put together one pretty good car then sold it dirt cheap. He rolled in money, but I didn't care about his wealth. I cared about him.

The second thing I cared about was horses. They didn't shout at me, they carried me on their backs and they loved the bags of barley I plucked for them. I was good at driving carts and all the time I dreamt I'd win the Big Bet. Then I'd have Grisha for a whole day.

He came to our house when my sister sang and never noticed when I sang.

He didn't know I swept the street in front of our porch for him. I knew the paths he preferred and I planted geraniums and lilac bushes there. Come on, somebody who knew our village would say. These paths are so steep lizards can't creep on them! That was true. It was difficult to plant lilac bushes on stone and make them survive in the heat. I carried pails and pails of water to the bushes and geraniums, and I left roses and bottles of cold lemonade for Grisha to find. He didn't notice me.

So one day—it was scorching hot, and the grass was motionless in the motionless air—I saw him pass, and I made up my mind. His hands were greasy, his face was greasy as well, and his eyes were indifferent. My heart became as small as a hazelnut.

"Grisha," I said as I jumped in front of him. "I am Anna and I am the daughter of Lila who casts lead bullets for faint-hearted kids, and sister of Pesho who drinks powerfully. Even you can't out-drink him. My father is the

guy who makes cornel brandy and you staggered and tee-
tered after you drank from it."

"I didn't teeter!" he said angrily.

"You did," I said. "But I didn't stop you to argue about
that." I felt something had gone wrong. His voice was
sharp and wrong too.

"So why did you stop me?" he said.

I had rehearsed two hundred times what I'd say to him,
but now when the time had come, my mouth felt dry like
the dust on the road that climbed the hill, and my tongue
was as heavy as the hill.

"Because I… I like you." It was true.

"All girls in the village of Staro like me," he remarked,
which made me angry.

I had picked roses for him and had trudged up the barren hill to bring lemonade for him.

"I want you to marry me," I said.

He stared. That made me so angry I could burst into
tears or into flames, which was all the same to me.

"Ha, ha!" he burst into laughter.

"Does 'Ha-ha!' mean 'yes'?" I said, boiling and seething. I didn't make cornel brandy, neither did I cast lead
bullets for faint-hearted kids, but I was Anna and I would
have no one laugh at me.

"I'd rather marry a worm than you," he said.

I looked at him. Yes, he was handsome, and he repaired
the jalopies of the entire district, and all the girls wanted
him, but I was Anna!

"Shall I take this is `No'? I said trying to appear calm.

"You understood me perfectly well," he said. "I won't marry you."

I was on the verge of saying there'd be no more roses strewn on the paths he chose to go for a walk, nor would he find bottles of lemonade left for him to drink, but I changed my mind.

"Good bye, Grisha," I said.

"Ha, ha," he laughed again.

"Don't say I have not asked you," I said as he turned his back on me and strode purposefully down the path.

"Ha, ha" his laughter echoed like a whip on a horse's back. And I knew how a horse felt after you whipped him.

But there would be a Big Bet again! Dad had brewed another barrel of cornel brandy. Well, why didn't anyone ask who'd picked the cornels, who sprinkled sugar on the mixture and who cleaned the cellar where the cornels took a century to ferment? It was me. I had thrown a lizard into the barrel and the brandy was sure to climb up your head like a lizard. The brew had a big kick in it because I kicked the barrel so many times that every cornel turned into a fist that would clout you across the side of the head.

The Big Bet day came and Dad announced it was Grisha who'd work a whole day for the winner.

"Come on, Anna," Mother said, "Go and pour out brandy for the guys. The whole village will participate in the race, so don't give them too much to drink."

"I'll pour no brandy into anybody's glasses, Mom," I said. "I'll participate in the race myself."

"What!" my mother said choking on her tongue. "A

woman can't drive a cart. Nobody's heard of such a stupid thing."

"You cast lead bullets and the kids are no longer afraid of anything in the world," I said. "But I need no bullet of yours. I want to win the Big Bet Race."

"No!" my brothers, the best rider and the best drinker in the village, said. "We won't give you a horse and we won't give you a cart. Shame on you, Anna!"

"I won't ask you to give me a cart and a horse," I said. "I'll go and take them myself."

"No!" Dad pointed out. "Look at your sister. She's meek as a calf and sings better than our TV. Why don't you try to sing like her?"

"Why don't you sing like her, Dad?" I said and he declared he was no TV and he was a brandy maker. Then he nodded shortly.

I knew what that meant. This had happened before. My two brothers, my mother, my father and my sister who was as meek as a calf sprang to their feet and surrounded me. My brothers threw a belt around my shoulders. Then Mother who was as strong as three men sat on my feet.

My meek sister tied my legs with the belt of her dress; my best drinking brother tied my arms with a piece of rope—the same one I had used when I dragged him from the pub to our one story house. Oh, no, he wasn't drunk, he had mumbled as I tugged him along. He wanted to prove how grand he was. Now my best riding brother tied me to the chair with an old bridle and said, "We are doing this for your own good. The carts will crush you like an egg and you'll die, then who else will go pick cornels for the brandy?"

"You are my favorite child," Dad said. "Everybody is somebody best among us. You are nobody and that saddens my heart."

"Here, drink some cornel brandy," my nightingale of a sister said. "Come on, drink that," she encouraged me. You'll fall asleep even before the guys put the horses to the carts. I'll sing for you and you won't suffer."

I felt like tearing up her nightingale ears and feeding them to the dogs.

Mother didn't say anything for a while, then suddenly she opened the window.

"You wailed like a lion when you were a baby," she said. "I sang to you and you howled louder. Your father and I danced for you to make you shut up. You wouldn't stop. You roared as if your tummy was full of vipers. Then I happened to open a window and you became as quiet as a worm. I've opened it for you now. So I hope you'll feel good, Anna."

Then my famous family, Father, Mother and all, went to the Big Bet. Dad had drunk enough so he burst into song and the minute he opened his mouth a glass fell from the table and my best riding brother dropped down on the floor—that was his trick to make Dad shut up. Alas, no success this time! The nightingale in the family, my sister, suddenly crooned too—that was how she hoped to discourage Dad's singing efforts. My drinking brother produced a bottle of brandy and tried to smuggle it to Dad, but Mother, I'd give her that, brandished the fire poker she'd grabbed from the hearth and roared, "Stop singing, man, or you'll be dead in an instant."

It was the poker that brought Dad back to sobriety and drove good sense into his head. He stopped roaring and rumbling, and said, "Whatever you say, sugar," to Mother.

"Sugar or no sugar, you'd better be quiet," my mother said pointedly as she took her black notebook. In it, she wrote down who drank from our cornel brandy and noted if the guy had to dig a cornfield, weed our peppers, or paint the walls of our kitchen to pay off his debts.

They all went out, leaving me tied like the old ox Mother had wanted slaughtered after a week. I was not an ox, so I started gnawing at the bridle with which my brother had tied me. Like everything else he had, that bridle was half rotten, and although the saliva in my mouth tasted bitter like the poison I often used to kill cockroaches, I gnawed the thing through and through. My hands were free.

I had no other cart but the old two-wheeled gig Dad kept in the back yard and drove the city folks with, showing them our beautiful countryside. Beautiful my foot! There were big sand hills that winds and heat had nibbled away over centuries. Waist-deep nettles were all over the place, thorns, hawthorns, thistles and elder trees flourished and burgeoned, and there were so many lizards crawling around that you stepped on them. The slopes were steep. Snakes and goats climbed the scorching hot outcrops of rocks, and dwarf cornel trees struck root in the cracks amidst the sandstones. The soil was so red that if you cut your finger no blood-red sand would spurt from your wound.

In the Big Bet, one had to drive his cart through the tract of red land from the top of Purple Hill and reach the bottom of Scarlet Gorge following the road in which the ruts were so deep you could swim in them if it was raining. I rushed to the gig and then I saw there was no horse left for me.

My best riding brother had taken Lightning, our huge stallion that would eat nothing but barley, so supercilious beast he was. My elder brother, the drinking talent, had taken our second horse, or should I say a limping ruin, but he'd already had a glass or two, and hobbling or limping horses made no difference to him. The nightingale, as always very special, rode the young colt Mother was to swap for a motorbike after the Big Bet was over. Mother's lead bullets had become so popular that after thinking and rethinking for a month, she made up her mind it was more advantageous for her to visit her patients riding a motorbike rather than a horse.

Marko, our scraggy obstinate donkey, happened to be the only living soul in sight. He was grazing dry yellow thistles in the backyard. If I had not found Marko, I'd have put our goat before the gig and I'd run for the Big Bet.

Marko, the gig, and I were the last to come to the venue of the competition. It was a dry meadow, all yellow grass and red sand under the hooves of the horses.

"Hey, look who's there!" the guys whistled, and the drinking talent, my younger brother, came up, grabbed my ear and pulled it very hard indeed. Then he spat on the gig and kicked the belly of the innocent donkey.

"Go home. Now," he hissed frothing at the mouth. "Our family will become the laughing stock of the district because of you."

I tried not to squirm.

"You go home," I hissed back. "My victory will be the talk of the district. And you will buy me a bike to glorify my achievement."

"Isn't she an idiot?" I heard my mother's comment.

Everybody guffawed.

"We are all democratic fellows here," Grisha, the bone-shaker repairer said. "Let her participate."

"I'll participate not because you say so, but because I want to," I snarled. "Mind you what I'll do to you after I win you for a day."

"Perhaps marry him?" a guy with a horse, as big as a hotel, said. "Are you beautiful enough?"

"I am," I said. "I'll do what I'll do."

The deep-rutted dirt road the competitors had to follow climbed down the red precipitous slope. The hill was cut and carved by three wild streams, all of which had run dry and gaped like mouths full of bad teeth. There were three narrow bridges over them, all shaky and rickety structures; then the carts had to cross the river at the foot of the hill. There was no water in it, just thick rich mud, overgrown with bulrush and teeming with water snakes, tadpoles and frogs. The old church—Saint Ivan Rilski the Miracle Maker—was on the opposite shore, in the middle of a flat patch of land, where we all gathered for Christmas and Easter to eat, drink and celebrate.

The track was narrow and tortuous, there were sharp stones that had wrenched wheels of carts before, and the rumble the hooves produced deafened young and all. Weeks after the Big Bet Mother couldn't hear Dad grumbling under his breath: a fact that suited the family fine. Dad usually sold two barrels of his brandy—which meant that Dad's buddies had to weed and sweep for Mother. As a rule, these guys were as industrious as mountain rocks. Like rocks, they wouldn't budge, and it was their wives who span for us, and knitted pullovers for the drinking talent, the nightingale and for me.

The carts were arranged in a row, all seven of them, my two talented brothers, the rider and the drunk, and five more guys. I was at the very end of the row, on a strip of land where there were more stones and lizards than air to breathe.

"Get out of my way!" the guy next to me said and kicked my donkey.

I kicked his horse in return and it was after the kick that Dad gave the signal. He whistled, waved his cap and all the seven carts rumbled down the hill, raising clouds of red dust and whirlwinds of sand. My gig, Marko, the donkey and I waited for the dust to settle. The onlookers: the nightingale, the housewives who had bet saucepans and teapots on their husbands, the girls who had bet their belts on their sweethearts, all shouted, "Hello, the laughingstock there! Waiting for Ivan the Miracle Maker to kick you?"

I had a plan, a daring and wild one. I wouldn't follow the dirt road. I'd take a shortcut through the dry brambles, briars, thistles and thorns I had so often roamed around picking cornels for dad's dangerous brandy. So I kicked Marko, trying to make him run though the dry grass, the spikes and barbs. The beast wouldn't budge so I kicked him much stronger. Off Marko went.

The gig hit sharp stones, briars and hawthorn bushes caught it, but the hill was as steep as a hanging rope, so the animal couldn't stop. My vehicle cut its way through dry nettles, Marko ran and brayed terrified, I shook, jumped and bounced, clutching the reins, seeing only Marko's tail and hooves. I didn't know what hit him, maybe a branch of a cornel tree, then something bit me, and another thing whipped and slapped me across the face. Marko whinnied, neighed and shrieked. He couldn't stop.

We thundered across the first dry stream and a flying stone clobbered me on the forehead. Then we roared and boomed across the second and third dry creeks, or did we? Small flies got into my eyes and bramble branches scratched my neck. Marco could not stop. Then suddenly there was mud everywhere around me, mud in my eyes and ears, and I could no longer see Marko's tail. The gig under me shook, wobbled, and rattled, something wet and slimy slid down my blouse. I didn't care.

"Saint Ivan Miracle Maker, help me!" I shouted.

Marko, the donkey, brayed for help too. *He's alive and kicking*—a happy thought crossed my mind and that was the last thing I remembered. In a haze, I saw one of the wheels fall off. Then the gig hit something hard, a snag, a rock, or a bone of a dead ox. The second wheel fell off. A wet muddy thing hit my nose. Marko brayed, trumpeted, pulled hard and flew downward with the wind. I fell, my back hit the ground, and I lay prostrate like a pair of cheap wet pants. I'm dead, I thought, but I wasn't. From the corner of my eye, I saw a big cross and a stone wall: I was in front of the church Saint Ivan the Miracle Maker. The gig, having lost all its wheels, drooped by my side, and Marko, the beast, all spluttered with mud, was licking my face with his wet cool tongue.

All my bones hurt. My nose bled and there was red mud in my mouth. The left sleeve of my blouse hung down my shoulder, a mere rag, and a frog jumped from it. There was no trace of the other sleeve. A slimy thing crawled out of my pants pocket and inched away creeping as best as it could up in the dust. A small water snake it was. Another grimy thing moved inside my blouse, slithering and hitting the skin of my belly. Briar branches and brambles hung from my hair.

I looked around. There was no other cart in front of the church Ivan the Miracle Maker. The saint had done a wonderful job at saving my and Marko's lives. On the other hand, he had thought it was beneath him to save the gig. As I watched, a side board of my vehicle broke up and fell onto the ground. Then I noticed all the other carts had stopped and the horses stood motionless in the heat. Competitors, their sweethearts, wives and mothers, neighbors, and children, all stared at me as silent as the empty pockets they all possessed. I tried to stand up, staggered and my nose landed in the dust.

"She's alive!" My mother shouted and all rushed to Ivan the Miracle Maker who stared modestly at the mud in the river from his beautiful icon in the church. I saw Grisha, the man with the nimblest hands in South Bulgaria, rush to me, and I thought of the mud in my hair, of the slippery thing that squirmed under my blouse. My head was as heavy as the gig and as shaken. Then I realized I had not reached the finishing line yet.

I scrambled to my feet, shook violently and fell. I scrambled to my feet again, grabbed one of the broken boards of the gig, and dragged it forward to the church. I wanted to win the race and win it honestly.

I pushed my way to the flat patch of land and collapsed in the middle of it. I'd reached the finishing line. I won. Then I spat mud in the dust and lay breathless on the yellow grass.

I was just trying to sit up when Dad reached out his hand to help me stand up. I disregarded it. I had something much more important on which to concentrate. Grisha was the second after Dad to reach me. He bent down and stared. His eyes looked terrified as he scrutinized my filthy feet, my mud-caked face and grimy hands.

"I got you," I said. "I won you and you are mine for a whole day."

"Priest Mano will refuse to proclaim you man and wife," my mother said, still panting. She had run from the top of the hill down to the church, and I was suddenly glad she was sweating profusely. She stopped speaking as she tried to get her wind. "No marriage is supposed to last less than a day."

The carters and their sweethearts, my brother, the drinking talent, and my elder brother, the rider, looked at me, their eyes burning.

"I'm proud of you!" the best rider said. "No one dared drive a gig through the Snake Gorge!"

"You flew over the crags! You drove Marko as if he were an angel!" my drinking brother said. "I love you, little sister. I love you!"

"I'll bring all faint-hearted and white-livered children to you," my mother said. "I'll let them touch the hem of your skirt and they'll never be afraid of anything in their lives."

The nightingale opened her mouth and a magnificent song poured out of it. This was the song about Ivan Rilski the Miracle Maker who, we believed, was born in our village. Then all of them, the carters and their sweethearts, their mothers, cousins and neighbors who had come to bet on the best cart, sang along. They shouted the words of the song, and they all stood motionless.

They sang for me.

They drank a lot, all of them, and my brother, the drinking talent, was proud they were his friends. Maybe the cornels were the reason their voices were so powerful, or maybe it was the river that made the tune rich, or the wind they breathed in was in the song. Their song was strong. My mother cast her lead bullets and was famous; my father brewed cornel brandy, and everyone in my family was known far and wide. But I was the first one, the only one in the whole village for whom the best carters sang the song about Ivan Rilski. They sang, and I tried to stand up. Finally, I scrambled to my feet and sang along. I loved the hill and the broken gig. As I bent to kiss Marko, the donkey, on the forehead, a slimy thing crawled out of my blouse and thudded on the red, caked earth. It was a big frog.

"What will you do to me?" the most beautiful voice asked me—Grisha's.

I thought about it. To be honest, I didn't even have to think about it. I knew.

"Dad has a big barrel in which he keeps the cornel brandy," I said. "I want you to climb on that barrel and stay there all day long."

"Why?" he breathed.

"All they long," I said. "I'll watch you."

The carters laughed, their sweethearts snickered and Dad growled, "You've got a screw loose. He can repair my old Ford instead."

"He can assemble the engine of my motorbike," the drinking talent ventured.

"No," I said. "I won him. He's mine for the day."

When everyone was quiet, Grisha, the expert mechanic and loudmouth, looked me straight in the eyes and said, "Well…if you ask me the same question which you asked me before the Big Bet began… my answer will be positive. You just have to ask me once more. And I'll say yes."

I looked him straight in the eyes and said, "No."

"Hey, nitwit, you've got him," my brother, the best rider, said.

"I don't ask the same question twice," I said.

"You are more obstinate than Marko the donkey," my nightingale of a sister said gruffly. "And you are less intelligent than him."

Everybody was quiet when the most beautiful voice, Grisha's, said, "Will you marry me, Anna?"

I couldn't believe the words I'd just heard.

"Anna, dearest," the most beautiful voice said.

I stole a look at Dad who was scratching his head, speechless. My mother, although she was a brave woman and cast bullets against fear for young and old, stared at me unbelieving.

"Will you become my wife, Anna?" Grisha said.

"I have to think about it," I said.

I knew what I'd say. I'd dreamed about it a thousand times. The gig had no wheels, and Marko was a sorry sight, all covered with mud, a couple of leeches gleaming like stickers on his back.

"Yes, Grisha, I will," I said. "But you'll climb atop that barrel and stand on it for an hour. Okay?"

Fomite
Burlington, Vermont

Fomite is a literary press whose authors and artists explore the human condition -- political, cultural, personal and historical -- in poetry and prose.

A fomite is a medium capable of transmitting infectious organisms from one individual to another.

"The activity of art is based on the capacity of people to be infected by the feelings of others." Tolstoy, *What is Art?*

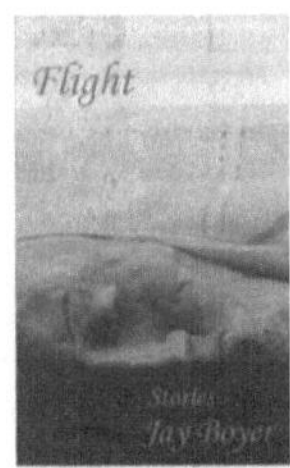

Flight and Other Stories - Jay Boyer
In *Flight and Other Stories,* we're with the fattest woman on earth as she draws her last breaths and her soul ascends toward its final reward. We meet a divorcee who can fly for no more effort than flapping her arms. We follow a middle-aged butler whose love affair with a young woman leads him first to the mysteries of bondage, and then to the pleasures of malice. Story by story, we set foot into worlds so strange as to seem all but surreal, yet everything feels familiar, each moment rings true. And that's when we recognize we're in the hands of one of America's truly original talents.

AlphaBetaBestiario - Antonello Borra
Animals have always understood that mankind is not fully at home in the world. Bestiaries, hoping to teach, send out warnings. This one, of course, aims at doing the same.

Loosestrife - Greg Delanty
These poems are a chronicle of complicity in our modern lives, a witnessing of war and the destruction of our planet. It is also an attempt to adjust the more destructive blueprint myths of our society. Often our cultural memory tells us to keep quiet about the aspects that are most challenging to our ethics, to forget the violations we feel and tremors that keep us distant and numb. If we begin to face and speak and create from these human aftermaths, as these poems do, then we can change and become more comfortable with healthier ways of being alive.

Fomite
Burlington, Vermont

Loisaida - Dan Chodorokoff
Catherine, a young anarchist estranged from her parents and squatting in an abandoned building on New York's Lower East Side is fighting with her boyfriend and conflicted about her work on an underground newspaper. After learning of a developer's plans to demolish a community garden, Catherine builds an alliance with a group of Puerto Rican community activists. Together they confront the confluence of politics, money, and real estate that rule Manhattan.   All the while she learns important lessons from her great-grandmother's life in the Yiddish anarchist movement that flourished on the Lower East Side at the turn of the century. In this coming of age story, family saga, and tale of urban politics, Dan Chodorkoff explores the "principle of hope," and examines how memory and imagination inform social change.

Still Time - Michael Cocchiarale
Still Time is a collection of twenty-five short and shorter stories exploring tensions that arise in a variety of contemporary relationships: a young boy must deal with the wrath of his out-of-work father; a woman runs into a man twenty years after an awkward sexual encounter; a wife, unable to conceive, imagines her own murder, as well as the reaction of her emotionally distant husband; a soon-to-be tenured English professor tries to come to terms with her husband's shocking return to the religion of his youth; an assembly line worker, married for thirty years, discovers the surprising secret life of his recently hospitalized wife. Whether a few hundred or a few thousand words, these and other stories in the collection depict characters at moments of deep crisis. Some feel powerless, overwhelmed—unable to do much to change the course of their lives. Others rise to the occasion and, for better or for worse, say or do the thing that might transform them for good. Even in stories with the most troubling of endings, there remains the possibility of redemption. For each of the characters, there is still time.

Improvisational Arguments - Anna Faktorovich
Improvisational Arguments is written in free verse to capture the essence of modern problems and triumphs. The poems clearly relate short, frequently humorous and occasionally tragic, stories about travels to exotic and unusual places, fantastic realms, abnormal jobs, artistic innovations, political objections, and misadventures with love.

Fomite
Burlington, Vermont

Carts and Other Stories - Zdravka Evtimova
Roots and wings are the key words that best describe the short story collection, *Carts and Other Stories,* by Zdravka Evtimova. The book is emotionally multilayered and memorable because of its internal power, vitality and ability to touch both the heart and your mind. Within its pages, the reader discovers new perspectives true wealth, and learns to see the world with different eyes. The collection lives on the borders of different cultures. *Carts and Other Stories* will take the reader to wild and powerful Bulgarian mountains, to silver rains in Brussels, to German quiet winter streets and to wind bitten crags in Afghanistan. This book lives for those seeking to discover the beauty of the world around them, and will have them appreciating what they have -- and perhaps what they have lost as well.

The Listener Aspires to the Condition of Music - Barry Goldensohn
"I know of no other selected poems that selects on one theme, but this one does, charting Goldensohn's career-long attraction to music's performance, consolations and its august, thrilling, scary and clownish charms. Does all art aspire to the condition of music as Pater claimed, exhaling in a swoon toward that one class act? Goldensohn is more aware than the late 19th century of the overtones of such breathing: his poems thoroughly round out those overtones in a poet's lifetime of listening."
John Peck, poet, editor, Fellow of the American Academy of Rome

When You Remember Deir Yassin - R.L Green
A collection of poems by an American Jewish writer, on the subject of the occupation and destruction of Palestine. Green comments: "Outspoken Jewish critics of Israeli crimes against humanity have, strangely, been called "anti-Semitic" as well as the hilariously illogical epithet "self-hating Jews." As a Jewish critic of the Israeli government, I have come to accept these accusations as a badge of honor, signifying my own fealty to a central element of Jewish identity and ethics: one must be a lover of truth and a friend to the oppressed, and stand with the victims of tyranny, not with the tyrants, despite tribal loyalty or self-advancement. These poems were written as expressions of outrage, and of grief, and to encourage my sisters and brothers of every cultural or national grouping to speak out against injustice, to try to save Palestine, and in so doing, to reclaim for myself my own place as part of the Jewish people."

Fomite
Burlington, Vermont

The Co-Conspirator's Tale - Ron Jacobs

There's a place where love and mistrust are never at peace; where duplicity and deceit are the universal currency. *The Co-Conspirator's Tale* takes place within this nebulous firmament. There are crimes committed by the police in the name of the law. Excess in the name of revolution. The combination leaves death in its wake and the survivors struggling to find justice in a San Francisco Bay Area noir by the author of the underground classic *The Way the Wind Blew: A History of the Weather Underground* and the novel *Short Order Frame Up*.

Roadworthy Creature, Roadworthy Craft -
Kate Magill

Words fail but the voice struggles on. The culmination of a decade's worth of performance poetry, *Roadworthy Creature, Roadworthy Craft* is Kate Magill's first full-length publication. In lines that are sinewy yet delicate, Magill's poems explore the terrain where idea and action meet, where bodies and words commingle to form a strange new flesh, a breathing text, an "I" that spirals outward from itself.

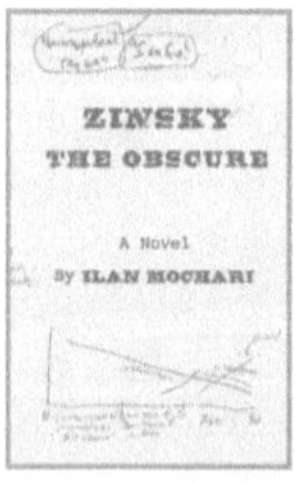

Zinsky the Obscure - Ilan Mochari

"If your childhood is brutal, your adulthood becomes a daily attempt to recover: a quest for ecstasy and stability in recompense for their early absence." So states the 30-year-old Ariel Zinsky, whose bachelor-like lifestyle belies the torturous youth he is still coming to grips with. As a boy, he struggles with the beatings themselves; as a grownup, he struggles with the world's indifference to them. *Zinsky the Obscure* is his life story, a humorous chronicle of his search for a redemptive ecstasy through sex, an entrepreneurial sports obsession, and finally, the cathartic exercise of writing it all down. Fervently recounting both the comic delights and the frightening horrors of a life in which he feels – always – that he is not like all the rest, Zinsky survives the worst and relishes the best with idiosyncratic style, as his heartbreak turns into self-awareness and his suicidal ideation into self-regard. A vivid evocation of the all-consuming nature of lust and ambition – and the forces that drive them – *Zinsky the Obscure* is a novel of extraordinary zeal, range, and power.

Fomite
Burlington, Vermont

The Derivation of Cowboys & Indians - Joseph D. Reich
The Derivation of Cowboys & Indians represents a profound journey, a breakdown of The American Dream from a social, cultural, historical, and spiritual point of view. Reich examines in concise!detail the loss of the collective unconscious, commenting on our contemporary postmodern culture with its self-interested excesses, on where and how things go wrong, and how social/political practice rarely meets its original proclamations and promises. Reich's surreal and self-effacing satire brings this troubling message home. *The Derivations of Cowboys & Indians* is a desperate search and struggle for America's literal, symbolic, and spiritual home.

Kasper Planet: - Peter Schumann
The British call him Punch, Italians, Pulchinello, Russians, Petruchka, Native Americans, Coyote. Every culture that worships authority will breed a Punch-like, anti-authoritan resister. Yin and yang -- it has to happen. The Germans call him Kasper.Truth-telling and serious pranking are dangerous professions when going up against power. Bradley Manning sits naked in solitary; Julian Assange is pursued by Interpol, Obama's Department of Justice, and Amazon.com. But -- in contrast to merely human faces -- masks and theater can often slip through the bars.Consider our American Kaspers: Charlie Chaplin, Woody Guthrie, Abby Hoffman, the Yes Men -- theater people all, utilizing various forms to seed critique. Their profiles and tactics have evolved along with those of their enemies. Who are the bad guys that call forth the Kaspers? Over the last half century, with his Bread & Puppet Theater, Peter Schumann has been tireless in naming them, excoriating them with Kasperdom....from Marc Estrin's Foreword to Planet Kasper

Views Cost Extra - L.E. Smith
Views that inspire, that calm, or that terrify – all come at some cost to the viewer. You will find a New Jersey high school preppy who wants to inhabit the "perfect" cowboy movie, a rural mailman disgusted with residents of his town who wants to live with penguins, an ailing screen writer who strikes a deal with Johnny Cash to reverse an old man's failures, an old man who ponders a young man's suicide attempt, a one-armed blind blues singer who wants to reunite with the car that took her arm on the assembly line -- and more. These stories suggest that we must pay something to live even ordinary lives.

Fomite
Burlington, Vermont

The Empty Notebook Interrogates Itself -

Susan Thomas

The Empty Notebook began its life as a very literal metaphor for a few weeks of what the poet thought was writer's block, but was really the struggle of an eccentric persona to take over her working life. It won. And for the next three years everything she wrote came to her in the voice of the Empty Notebook, who, as the notebook began to fill itself, became rather opinionated, changed gender, alternately acted as bully and victim, had many bizarre adventures in exotic locales and developed a somewhat politically-incorrect attitude. It then began to steal the voices and forms of other poets and tried to immortalize itself in various poetry reviews. It is now thrilled to collect itself in one slim volume.

My God, What Have We Done? - Susan Weiss

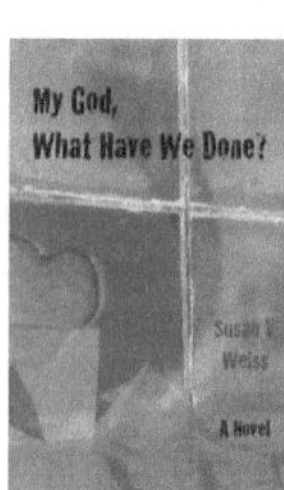

In a world afflicted with war, toxicity, and hunger, does what we do in our private lives really matter? Fifty years after the creation of the atomic bomb at Los Alamos, newlyweds Pauline and Clifford visit that once-secret city on their honeymoon, compelled by Pauline's fascination with Oppenheimer, the soulful scientist. The two stories emerging from this visit reverberate back and forth between the loneliness of a new mother at home in Boston and the isolation of an entire community dedicated to the development of the bomb. While Pauline struggles with unforeseen challenges of family life, Oppenheimer and his crew reckon with forces beyond all imagining.

Finally the years of frantic research on the bomb culminate in a stunning test explosion that echoes a rupture in the couple's marriage. Against the backdrop of a civilization that's out of control, Pauline begins to understand the complex, potentially explosive physics of personal relationships.

At once funny and dead serious, *My God, What Have We Done?* sifts through the ruins left by the bomb in search of a more worthy human achievement.